The Mystery of the Screaming Clock

D1189000

This Armada book belongs to:

_____

_____

_____

Alfred Hitchcock and
The Three Investigators
in

The Mystery of the Screaming Clock

Text by Robert Arthur

Armada

First published in the U.K. in 1969 by
William Collins Sons & Co. Ltd., London and Glasgow.
This edition was first published in Armada in 1971 by
Fontana Paperbacks,
14 St. James's Place, London SW1A 1PF.

This impression 1978.

Printed in Great Britain by Love & Malcomson Ltd.,
Brighton Road, Redhill, Surrey.

A Few Words From Alfred Hitchcock

Greetings and salutations! It is a pleasure to have you join me for another adventure with that remarkable trio of lads who call themselves The Three Investigators. This time a most unusual screaming clock leads them into a tangled web of clues, mystery and excitement.

I imagine that you have already met The Three Investigators and know that they are Jupiter Jones, Bob Andrews and Pete Crenshaw, all of Rocky Beach, California, a small community on the shores of the Pacific not far from Hollywood. But just in case this is your first meeting with the three, let me add that they make their Headquarters in a mobile home trailer cleverly hidden from sight in The Jones Salvage Yard. This fabulous junkyard is owned by Jupiter's aunt and uncle, for whom the trio work to earn spending money when they are not busy with their investigations.

Enough of introductions. On with the case! The clock is about to scream!

ALFRED HITCHCOCK

1

The Clock Screams

THE CLOCK SCREAMED.

It was the scream of a woman in mortal terror. It started at a low pitch, then went higher and higher until it hurt Jupiter's ears. A shiver ran down his back. It was the most terrifying sound he had ever heard.

And yet it was just an old-fashioned electric alarm clock. Jupiter had merely plugged it in to see if it would run. The next thing he knew it was screaming at him.

Jupiter grabbed the clock's electric cord and pulled it out of the socket. The scream stopped. Jupiter let out his breath with a gasp of relief. The sound of a clock screaming like a woman had been rather unnerving.

Running feet sounded behind him. Bob Andrews and Pete Crenshaw, who had been working in the front part of The Jones Salvage Yard, skidded to a stop beside him.

"Golly, what was that?" Bob asked.

"Are you hurt, Jupe?" Pete peered at him anxiously.

7

Jupiter shook his head.

"Listen," he said. "I want you to hear something rather unusual."

He plugged in the clock again, and once more the terrifying scream filled the air. He pulled out the plug and the scream stopped instantly.

"Wow!" Pete said. "A clock that screams, and he calls it *rather* unusual!"

"I wonder what he'd say if it grew wings and flew away?" Bob grinned. "Maybe then he'd say it was *quite* unusual. As far as I'm concerned a screaming clock is almost the most unusual thing I've ever bumped into."

Jupiter ignored their friendly sarcasm. He was turning the clock over in his hands, studying it. Then he said, in a tone of satisfaction, "Ah!"

"Ah, what?" Pete demanded.

"The alarm lever is at *On*," Jupiter told them. "I'll shut it off and plug the clock in again."

He did this and the clock began to purr softly. It made no other sound.

"Now let's see what happens." Jupiter flipped the alarm lever to *On*. Instantly the clock screamed again. Jupiter quickly switched it off.

"Well," he said, "we've solved the first part of the mystery. The clock screams instead of ringing an alarm."

"What mystery?" Pete demanded. "What mystery have we solved the first part of?"

Jupe means a screaming clock is certainly a

mystery," Bob said. "And he's solved why it screams."

"Not why," Jupiter corrected him. "Just when. The clock screams when the alarm is set. *Why* it does is a much better mystery. I have a feeling it will be an interesting one to investigate."

"What do you mean, investigate?" Pete asked. "How can you investigate a clock? Ask it questions? Give it the third degree?"

"A clock that screams when it should ring an alarm is certainly mysterious," Jupiter answered. "And the motto of The Three Investigators is——"

"We investigate anything!" Bob and Pete answered together.

"All right," Pete went on. "So it's a mystery. I still want to know how you can investigate it."

"By finding out why it was made to scream. There must be a reason for it," Jupiter told him. "We haven't any other mystery on hand right now, so I propose we get some good practice by investigating this screaming clock."

"Oh no!" Pete groaned. "We have to draw the line somewhere."

But Bob looked interested. "How would you start, Jupe?" he asked.

Jupiter reached for his tool kit, which was in a drawer of a nearby workbench. The boys were in Jupe's workshop section of The Jones Salvage

9

Yard, owned and run by his uncle and aunt, Titus and Mathilda Jones. Here, hidden from the eyes of curious adults by piles of junk, they could work undisturbed.

To one side of them was the big pile of miscellaneous salvage material—steel beams, lumber, crates, an old playground chute—which they had carefully arranged to hide the small mobile home trailer that was Headquarters for The Three Investigators. They could get into it only through certain secret entrances too small for an adult. At the moment, however, they had no need to go inside.

Jupiter took out a screwdriver and began to remove the back of the clock. He slipped it down along the electric wire so that he could peer inside. For the second time he said, "Ah!" He pointed with the screwdriver to something that had apparently been added to the interior of the clock. It was a disc about as large as a silver dollar, but thicker.

"I believe this is the mechanism that produces the scream," he said. "Someone very clever at mechanics has installed it in place of the regular alarm bell."

"But why?" Bob asked.

"That's the mystery. To start investigating it, first we have to learn who did the work."

"I don't see how we can do that," Pete protested.

"You're not thinking like an investigator," Jupiter said. "Now put your mind to it. Tell me how you would begin with this mystery."

"Well—first I suppose I'd try to find out where the clock came from."

"Correct. And how would you go about that?"

"Well, the clock came into the salvage yard as junk," Pete said. "So I guess your Uncle Titus bought it. Maybe he remembers where he got it."

"Mr. Jones buys an awful lot of things," Bob said doubtfully. "He doesn't always keep track of where he got them."

"True," agreed Jupiter. "But Pete is right. The first thing to do is ask Uncle Titus if he knows where the clock came from. He gave it to me just half an hour ago in a box of odds and ends. Now let's see what else is in the box."

A cardboard carton sat on his workbench. Jupiter reached in and pulled out a stuffed owl with most of the feathers falling out. Underneath it was a clothesbrush, badly worn. Then came a broken goose-neck lamp, a vase with a chip in it, a pair of book ends made to look like horses' heads, and several other knick-knacks, most of them broken and all equally valuable— or useless, whichever way you chose to look at it.

"It looks to me," Jupiter remarked, "as if

someone cleaned out a lot of old stuff, put it in a box and threw it away. Then some refuse collector rescued it and sold the box to Uncle Titus. Uncle Titus will buy almost anything if the price is right. He counts on our ability to fix things so they can be sold again."

"I wouldn't give you a dollar for the lot," Pete said. "Except the clock. It seems like a good clock. Except for that scream when the alarm is turned on. Imagine waking up with that scream ringing in your ears!"

"Hmm." Jupiter looked thoughtful. "Suppose you wanted to frighten someone badly. Perhaps even scare them to death. So you slipped this clock into their bedroom in place of their regular clock, and the next morning when the alarm went off a fatal heart attack followed. That would certainly be a clever murder plot."

"Gosh!" Bob said. "You think that's what happened?"

"I haven't any idea," Jupiter answered. "I just suggested it as a possibility. Now let's go ask Uncle Titus if he knows where the clock came from."

He led the way from the workshop area to the little cabin in the front of the salvage yard which served as an office. Hans and Konrad, the two husky Bavarian yard helpers, were busy stacking usable building material in neat piles. Titus Jones a small man with an enormous moustache

12

and bright, twinkling eyes, was inspecting some used furniture.

"Well, boys?" Mr. Jones said as they approached. "Any time you want to make some spending money I've got a batch of furniture here that can use fixing up and painting."

"We'll get to it soon, Uncle Titus," Jupiter promised. "Right now we're interested in this clock. It was in that box of odds and ends you gave me to look over. Can you tell us where the box came from?"

"Hmm." Titus Jones thought deeply. "Got it from somebody. Didn't pay for it. Fellow threw it in with this furniture I bought. He's a refuse collector, up Hollywood way. Goes around salvaging stuff people put out for collection. Sells whatever has any value. Lots of people throw away good used stuff, you know."

"Do you know his name, Uncle Titus?"

"Just his first name. Tom. That's all. Expect him to drop in this morning with another load. You could ask him then."

At that moment an old pickup truck pulled into the yard, and a whiskery man wearing overalls hopped out.

"By gravy, here he is now," said Mr. Jones. "Good morning, Tom."

"Morning, Titus," he said. "Got some furniture for you. Real good stuff. Almost new."

"You mean it isn't old enough to be antique

13

yet." Titus Jones chuckled. "Give you ten dollars for the lot without looking at it."

"Taken," Tom said promptly. "Want me to unload it here?"

"Over behind the office. First, Jupiter here wants to ask you something."

"Sure thing. Shoot, boy."

"We're trying to trace a boxful of things you gave Uncle Titus," Jupiter said. "It had this clock in it, for one thing. We thought you might remember."

"Clock?" Tom chuckled. "I pick up a dozen clocks a week. Throw most of them away. Can't remember a clock."

"The box also had a stuffed owl in it," Bob spoke up. "Maybe you remember the owl."

"Owl? Owl? That rings a bell. Remember picking up a box with a stuffed owl in it. Don't pick up many stuffed owls. I remember that one, all right. It was in back of some house in—now just give me a minute, it'll come to me. It was in . . ."

Tom shook his head.

"Sorry, boy. It was at least two weeks ago. Had it in my garage ever since. I plain can't remember where I picked up that box of stuff."

2

Jupiter Finds a Clue

"WELL, that was one investigation that stopped even before it got started," Pete remarked. "Since we can't trace the clock, we can't possibly find out— What are you doing, Jupe?"

They were back in the workshop and Jupiter was turning over in his hands the empty cardboard box which held the screaming clock.

"Sometimes a box will have an address on it," he said. "The address it was delivered to."

"It looks like just a grocery carton to me," Bob said.

"You're right. There's no address on the box."

"Then as I said," Pete continued, "this is one investigation—What are you doing, Bob?"

Bob was picking up a rectangular piece of paper that had fluttered beneath the printing press.

"This fell out of the box," he told Jupiter. "It has some writing on it."

"Probably just a grocery list," Pete said. But he crowded closer to Bob. There were only a few words, written in ink, and Jupe read them aloud.

Dear Rex:
Ask Imogene.
Ask Gerald.
Ask Martha.
Then act! The result will surprise even you.

"Good grief!" Bob exclaimed. "What is that supposed to mean?"

"Ask Gerald!" Pete groaned. "Ask Imogene! Ask Martha! Who are these characters and what are we supposed to ask them? And why?"

"I would guess this is all part of the mystery of the clock," Jupiter said.

"Why do you say that?" Bob asked. "It's just a slip of paper that was in the box. How do we know it has any connection with the clock?"

"I think it has," Jupiter told them. "Observe the paper. It has been trimmed with scissors to a certain size—about two inches wide by four inches long. Now look at the back. What do you see?"

"Looks like some dried glue," Bob said.

"Exactly. This slip of paper has been glued to something. Now let's look at the clock. On the bottom there's a space just large enough for the paper. When I put the two together the paper fits perfectly. I run my finger over the bottom of the clock, and I feel something rough. I deduce that it is also dried glue. So the answer is simple. This piece of paper was originally glued to the bottom of the screaming clock, and it fell off when the clock was rattling around in the box."

"But why would anybody glue a crazy message like that to the bottom of a clock?" Pete wanted to know. "It doesn't make sense."

"A mystery wouldn't be a mystery if it wasn't mysterious," Jupiter told him.

"I'll buy that," Pete remarked. "Well, now we've doubled the mystery, and we're back where we started from. We still can't trace the clock and—What are you doing now, Jupe?"

"I'm scratching the dried glue off the bottom of the clock. There seems to be something under it. It's engraving, but it's too small to read and there is glue in the letters. Let's move into Headquarters and get a magnifying glass."

He stepped behind the printing press, moved aside a metal grating that just seemed to be leaning there, and uncovered the entrance to a large corrugated pipe. One after another, they crawled through the pipe, which was about thirty feet long and padded with old rugs so they wouldn't bang their knees. This was Tunnel Two. It ran partly underground and brought them directly beneath the mobile home trailer which was Headquarters.

Jupiter pushed up a trapdoor. They all scrambled into the tiny office of Headquarters, which had been fitted up some time ago with a desk, a small filing cabinet, a typewriter, a tape recorder and a telephone. Jupe flipped on the overhead light and took a large magnifying glass from the desk drawer. He studied the base of the electric alarm clock, nodded, and held it out to Bob.

Bob peered through the glass and saw, engraved into the metal base of the clock, a name in very tiny letters—*A. Felix*.

"What does it mean?" he asked.

"I'll tell you in a minute, I think," Jupiter said. "Pete, hand me the telephone book. The classified section."

He took the phone book containing the classified advertising and began to turn the pages. Then he gave an exclamation of triumph.

"Look!" he said.

Under the heading CLOCKMAKERS there was an advertisement. It said: *A. Felix—Clockmaker —Unusual Jobs Our Specialty*. This was followed by a Hollywood address and a telephone number.

"Clockmakers," Jupiter informed them, "often engrave a code number on a watch or clock they fix. That helps them identify it if it comes in again. Or they sometimes engrave their name on a job they're very proud of. I think we have found out who fixed the clock so it would scream. That's the first step in our investigation.

"The next step is to go ask Mr. Felix who hired him to do the job."

3

On the Trail

THE SHOP OF *A. Felix—Clockmaker* turned out
to be a narrow store on a side-street off Hollywood Boulevard, Hollywood's famous main
thoroughfare.

"You may park here, Worthington," said
Jupiter to the English chauffeur who had just
driven them from Rocky Beach. Jupiter had won
the use of Worthington and a superb antique
Rolls-Royce some time before, as a result of win-
ning a contest conducted by the Rent-'n-Ride
Agency. The time during which he could use the
car had recently expired, however, and the boys
had been afraid they could not continue as investigators without this means of covering the
vast distances of southern California. But because of the generosity of August August, a boy
for whom they had located a valuable inherit-
ance, they again had use of the fabulous car and
chauffeur.

"Very good, Master Jupiter," replied the dig-
nified Englishman. He parked the car, and the
three boys got out.

They peered into a dusty, narrow shop window with the name *A. Felix—Clockmaker* lettered on it in peeling gold paint. The window was full of clocks, large and small, new and antique, plain ones and clocks ornately decorated with birds and flowers. As they watched, a door in a tall wooden clock opened and a toy bugler marched out, lifted his bugle, and blew several times to indicate the hour.

"That's pretty neat," Pete observed. "I'd rather be bugled at than screamed at."

"Let's go in and see if Mr. Felix can tell us anything," Jupiter said.

As they entered the shop they were confused by a loud buzz, as of millions of bees. Then they realized it was the sound of many clocks, maybe a hundred or more, all ticking away together.

A tiny man in a leather apron came towards them down an aisle crowded with clocks. He had bushy white eyebrows and sparkling black eyes.

"Are you looking for something special in a clock?" Mr. Felix asked cheerfully. "Or perhaps it's just a broken watch you wish me to fix?"

"No, sir," Jupiter replied. "We wanted to consult you about this clock."

He opened the zipper bag he carried and took out the screaming clock.

Mr. Felix studied it for a moment.

"A rather old electric alarm clock," he said. "Of little value. I do not believe it is worth fixing."

"It doesn't need fixing, sir," Jupiter said. "Plug it in, if you don't mind."

The tiny man shrugged. He plugged in the clock.

"Now turn on the alarm, sir," Jupiter requested.

Mr. Felix did. Instantly the terrifying scream filled the little shop. Mr. Felix hurriedly moved the small knob on the back of the clock. The scream died away to a mere whisper. Mr. Felix picked up the clock and studied the back. He smiled.

"I remember this clock now," he said. "That was a tricky job, though no more tricky than others I have done."

"Then you made the clock scream?" Pete asked.

"Yes, I did. An ingenious mechanism, wouldn't you say? But I am afraid I cannot tell you for whom I did it. All work that I do is confidential."

"Yes, sir," Jupiter said. "But you see, this clock was found thrown out in some trash. It must have been an accident. The owner obviously paid you a lot of money to make it scream for him, and he can't have meant to throw it away. We'd like to return it."

"I see," said Mr. Felix thoughtfully.

"We were hoping there might be a reward," Bob put in.

Mr. Felix shrugged and plugged in the clock.

Mr. Felix nodded. "Well, that's perfectly proper. Yes, it must have been discarded by accident. The clock works perfectly well. Under the circumstances I believe that I can tell you as much as I am able. The name of the customer for whom I did the work was Clock."

"Clock?" Bob and Pete repeated the word in surprise.

"He called himself A. Clock. Of course I always thought he was making a joke because he brought me a number of clocks to work on from time to time."

"It doesn't sound like a real name," Jupiter mused. "But if he gave you his address, it wouldn't matter. We could go there anyway."

"Unfortunately, he just gave me a telephone number. Still, you could call him."

He popped behind a counter and brought out a big record book. He turned a few pages, and stopped.

"A. Clock," he read, "Telephone number——" And he gave a number which Bob, as record keeper, jotted down in a notebook.

"Can you tell us anything else, sir?" Jupiter asked. Mr. Felix shook his head.

"That's all," he said. "Perhaps I have said too much. Now excuse me, I have work to do. Time is precious, young gentlemen, and must be used well. Good-bye."

He scurried off. Jupiter squared his shoulders.

"Well, we've made some progress," he said. "Now we'll go out and telephone that number. I saw a telephone booth at the corner."

"What are you going to say?" Pete asked as Jupiter was entering the booth.

"I'm going to use strategy to get the address," Jupe replied.

Bob and Pete squeezed in with him so they could listen to the conversation. The First Investigator dropped in a coin and dialled the number. After a moment a woman's voice answered.

"Good afternoon," Jupiter said, making his voice deep enough to sound like an adult. Jupe had a lot of acting ability, which he occasionally put to good use. "This is the telephone company calling. We are having trouble with crossed circuits."

"Crossed circuits? I don't understand," the woman answered.

"We have had complaints of parties in your section getting wrong numbers," Jupiter said. "Could you tell me the address from which you are answering? It will help us check the circuits."

"The address? Why, this is 309 Franklin Street. But I don't see how——"

She was interrupted by a scream. It was a deep-voiced scream, as of a large man terribly frightened. All three boys would have jumped

24

at the sound if they hadn't been wedged into the phone booth so tightly.

Then the phone went dead.

4

The Screaming Grandfather

"THIS MUST BE the block, Worthington," Jupiter said. "Drive slowly and we'll look for the right number."

"Very good, Master Jones," Worthington agreed. He drove slowly down Franklin Street. It was in the older part of town, once fashionable, and the houses that lined it were large, though somewhat run-down.

"There it is!" Pete cried.

Worthington stopped at the kerb. The boys climbed out and started up the walk, eyeing the house with interest. The shades were pulled down and the house almost seemed abandoned. There were two steps to the front door. The boys climbed them and Jupiter rang the bell.

For a long time nothing happened. Then the

door creaked open. A woman stood there. She was not very old but she looked tired and unhappy.

"Excuse me," Jupiter said. "May we speak to Mr. Clock?"

"Mr. Clock?" The woman seemed puzzled. "There's nobody here by that name."

"Perhaps that isn't his real name," Jupiter said. "But he's someone interested in clocks. And he lives here. Or at least he used to."

"Interested in clocks? You must mean Mr. Hadley. But Mr. Hadley is——"

"Don't tell them anything," a voice suddenly broke in, and a black-haired boy of about seventeen pushed in front of the woman. He scowled at The Three Investigators. "Don't even talk to them, Mom. Shut the door. They have no business coming here and asking questions."

"Now, Harry," his mother reproved the boy. "That's not polite. They seem like perfectly nice boys and they're looking for Mr. Hadley. At least I guess it's Mr. Hadley."

"Was it Mr. Hadley who screamed a few minutes ago?" Jupiter asked unexpectedly.

The boy glared at him. "Yes, it was!" he replied loudly. "That was his dying scream. Now you better get away from here, because we have to bury Mr. Hadley."

With that he slammed the door shut.

"Did you hear that?" Pete exclaimed.

26

"They've killed somebody and now they have to bury him!"

"Hadn't we better call the police?" Bob asked.

"Not yet," Jupiter said. "We need more facts. We have to try to get into this house."

"You mean break in?" Bob asked

"No." Jupe shook his head. "We have to get these people to let us in. I see Harry peeking through the window beside the door. I'm going to ring again."

He rang, hard. The door flew open.

"I said to go away!" Harry shouted. "We don't want anybody bothering us."

"We don't want to bother you," Jupiter said quickly. "We're investigating a mystery and we'd like your help. Look, here's our business card."

He whipped out one of the cards all three carried. Harry took it and looked at it. It said:

THE THREE INVESTIGATORS

"We Investigate Anything"

?   ?   ?

First Investigator – JUPITER JONES
Second Investigator – PETER CRENSHAW
Records and Research – BOB ANDREWS

"What are the question marks for?" Harry

sneered. "Do they mean you don't know what you're doing?"

"They stand for mysteries unsolved, riddles unanswered, puzzles of any kind," Jupiter said. "Our motto is right there, 'We Investigate Anything.' Right now we're investigating a very strange clock. See, here it is."

He brought out the clock and handed it to Harry. Curiosity made the boy look it over.

"What's so mysterious about it?" Harry demanded.

"We'll demonstrate if you'll let us use an electric socket," Jupiter said.

He stepped forward as if certain that Harry would let him in. Harry stood aside and they entered a dark, narrow hallway, with stairs on one side going up to the second floor. On the other side was a big grandfather clock, going tick-tock, tick-tock. Beside the clock was a table with a telephone.

Bob and Pete peered around for the body of the mysterious Mr. Hadley, but they saw nothing. Jupiter spotted an electricity point beside the grandfather clock.

"I'll just plug the clock in here," he said, "and now I'll switch on the alarm lever and—listen!"

The clock screamed again. Its eerie wail in the dark hall brought out goose-pimples on Pete and Bob.

"There" Jupiter said, unplugging the clock.

"Wouldn't you say that's a mysterious clock worth investigating?"

"Nope!" Harry answered rudely. "Anyone can make a clock scream. Listen and I'll show you."

He reached behind the grandfather clock and pulled out an electric cord. He plugged it in and their hair stood on end as a man's deep voice rose in a scream, then faded away, as if he were falling over a high cliff.

The grandfather clock had screamed! This must be what they had heard over the telephone earlier.

The woman came hurrying out of a back room.

"Harry, for goodness sake, what——" she began. Then she saw The Three Investigators. "Oh," she said in confusion, "you let them in. What are you doing, Harry? What do they want here?"

"They have a screaming clock," Harry said as he pulled out the electric cord. "A little one. I never saw it before but it must have been Mr. Hadley's."

He took the clock from the table and handed it to his mother. She shook her head.

"No, I never saw it before," she said. "You're sure it was Mr. Hadley's?"

"Positive, Mom," Harry said. "Nobody else

would have a clock fixed so it would scream, would they?"

"No," his mother shook her head. "I guess not. But where did these boys get it?"

"I don't know yet," Harry said, still sounding almost angry but more friendly than he had been. "They're some kind of investigators and since they have one of Mr. Hadley's clocks I figured I might as well see what they want."

He opened a door and gestured for the three to go through it. They found themselves in a spacious library with panelled walls. On the walls were several framed oil paintings and at the other end of the room was a large mirror which reflected them and made the room seem bigger. There were shelves from floor to ceiling containing hundreds of books.

But what they noticed most were the clocks. There were a dozen or more of them in the room, some standing on the floor like the grand-father clock, others on tables and shelves. They all seemed old and valuable. Apparently they had all been electrified, as they didn't tick, but merely hummed.

"You see those clocks?" Harry demanded. "Well, I'll tell you something. Every one of them screams."

5

The Room of Clocks

THE ROOM WAS SCREAMING.

First it gave a high-pitched wail, like a frightened baby. Then it bellowed like a furiously angry man. Next it changed to a wild, animal-like cry which was the scream of a panther. Then from all sides came wails, screams, shrieks, bellows and animal snarls that blended into the most frightening sound any of the boys had ever heard. They sat side by side on a couch, cold chills running down their backs, and listened.

Harry sat at a desk, manipulating a set of switches to make the room scream. It was now apparent to The Three Investigators that all of the clocks in the room were equipped with screaming devices, probably similar to that in their alarm clock, and Harry was making them scream one by one and all together, with the ease of much practice.

He grinned at them, enjoying their amazement, and finally turned all the switches off, letting the room become silent.

"Bet you never heard anything like that before," he said. "You can see why your clock didn't mean anything to me. I'm used to clocks screaming."

"Is this room soundproofed?" Jupiter asked. "If it isn't, the neighbours will certainly be calling the police by now."

"Of course it's soundproofed," Harry said loftily. "This is Mr. Hadley's screaming room. He used to sit here at night and make all the clocks scream. He taught me how to do it before he—anyway, he taught me."

"Did something happen to Mr. Hadley?" Jupiter asked.

"No, of course not. Why should it?" Harry flared up.

"You started to say, 'before he——,' then you stopped. I thought you might have been going to say something happened to him."

"He went away, that's all. What's it to you, anyway?"

"We started out to investigate a screaming clock," Jupiter said. "Now we've run into a whole roomful of screaming clocks. It seems to me we have a much bigger mystery. Why should anyone have so many clocks fixed so they could scream like people and animals? It just doesn't make sense."

"I'll buy a double helping of that," Pete agreed. "It's about as wacky as anything I ever heard of."

"It was Mr. Hadley's hobby." Harry was defensive now. "A hobby doesn't have to make sense. He wanted a hobby nobody else had and he collected screaming clocks. What's your hobby?" He shot the final question at Jupiter.

"Solving mysteries," Jupe said. "Like this one."

"I tell you there isn't any mystery here!"

"Well, maybe there isn't a mystery but something's bothering you. You act as if you hate everybody. Why not tell us about it? Maybe we could help somehow."

"How could you help?" Harry flared up. "I mean, there's nothing bothering me. Except you guys. You're bothering me. Now why don't you get out and leave me alone."

He ran to the door and opened it.

"This way out!" he said. "And don't come back because—oh!" He broke off suddenly. The front door of the house had opened and a large man was coming in. He was not too tall, but he was very broad across the shoulders. He looked at Harry, then stared at the three boys. He scowled.

"What's this, Harry?" he demanded. "You've brought friends in the house to play, to make a lot of noise, to upset me? You know I must have absolute quiet."

"We aren't making any noise, Mr. Jeeters,"

B

Harry said, his tone sullen. "Anyway, this room is soundproof."

The big man gave Bob, Pete and Jupiter a long look, as if memorizing their appearance.

"I'll have to have a little talk with your mother," he said.

He went on up the stairs.

"What's he got against you bringing anybody in the house?" Bob asked, puzzled. "It's your house, isn't it?"

"No, it's Mr. Hadley's house," Harry said. "My mom is the housekeeper. We've been living here since Mr. Hadley went away, and we rent the upstairs floor to Mr. Jeeters because we have to have money to keep the house running. Now you'd better get going. You've caused enough trouble as it is."

"All right," Jupiter said. "Come on, Bob, Pete. Thanks for showing us the other screaming clocks, Harry."

He led the way out into the hall, where he picked up their own screaming alarm clock from the telephone table. He stowed it in the zipper bag and they all went out to where Worthington had the car parked.

"Well, we didn't get very far with this investigation," Pete grumbled as they climbed into the car. "I guess a man can collect screaming clocks if he wants to. That's the end of your mystery, Jupe."

"I suppose so," Jupiter agreed. He spoke to the chauffeur. "We're in Hollywood, Worthington, so let's stop at World Studios and ask if Mr. Hitchcock can see us. He might be interested in our clock."

"Very good, Master Jupiter," replied Worthington. He started the car.

"Wait a minute, Worthington," said Bob suddenly.

Harry Smith was running down the walk from the house. Pete rolled down the rear window and Harry leaned in, breathing hard.

"I'm glad I caught you," he said. "I've made up my mind. You're investigators and maybe you can help after all. My dad's in jail for something he didn't do and I want you to help me prove he's innocent."

6

More Mystery

"GET IN THE CAR, Harry, and tell us about it," Jupiter said. "Then we'll have an idea whether we can help you or not."

Harry squeezed in with them. His story didn't take long to tell. About three years before, he and his father and mother had come to live at Mr. Hadley's home. In return for an apartment at the back of the house and a small salary, Harry's mother acted as housekeeper for Mr. Hadley, who wasn't married. Harry's father was a life insurance salesman who was struggling to build up a business.

He had been starting to do fairly well Then, six months ago, there had been a robbery in the home of a businessman in nearby Beverly Hills. Three very valuable modern paintings had been cut from their frames by a thief who had either squeezed in through a very small window, or else had had a duplicate key to the front door.

The police had learned that Ralph Smith, Harry's father, had visited the house from which the pictures were stolen just a couple of weeks before. He had been trying to sell the owner a life insurance policy. Of course he had seen the pictures, but he claimed he knew nothing about art and hadn't known they were valuable.

Just because he had been in the house, the police searched the Smiths' apartment. And spread out underneath the linoleum in the kitchen they had found the stolen pictures. They had arrested Harry's father, and at his trial he was found guilty and sentenced to five years in prison. That had been three months ago. Harry's father had protested his innocence to the very end, saying he had no idea where the stolen pictures had come from. However, the jury had found him guilty.

"And he didn't do it!" Harry finished. "My dad isn't a criminal. Mom and I'd know it if he was. Now the police think he's the one who's been stealing art treasures all over the city for the last ten years—just because he's an insurance salesman who is out a lot at night calling on people.

"So I want to hire you to help me. I can't pay you much because I've only got fifteen dollars in my savings bank, but it's all yours if you can do anything for my father."

Jupiter blinked, thinking about it. Bob and Pete looked blank. The way they figured it, the police had to be pretty positive to send anyone to jail.

"It's a very difficult case, Harry," Jupiter said at last. "There doesn't seem to be much to work on."

"If it was easy I wouldn't need investigators to help me!" Harry flared up. "You carry cards saying you're investigators! Well, let's see you prove it. Do some investigating!"

Jupiter pinched his lower lip, which always helped put his mental machinery in high gear.

"We'll do some thinking about it, anyway," he agreed. "But if your father didn't steal the paintings, how did they get underneath the linoleum in your kitchen?"

"I don't know." There was misery in Harry's voice as he spoke. "Mr. Hadley had a lot of visitors who came and went. Maybe one of them hid them there. Or someone who wanted to get even with my dad for something could have broken into the house late at night and hidden the paintings where they would be found."

"Didn't you keep the back door locked?" Bob asked.

"Sure, but it's an old house and an old lock. Easy to open. We never worried because there wasn't anything worth stealing in our apartment."

"Hmmm." Jupiter was still pinching his lip. "Notice that the paintings were slipped under the kitchen linoleum, the first handy place anyone would come to if they got in through the back door. They could hide them there and get away without coming any farther into the house."

"That's good thinking, Jupe," Pete declared. "I'll bet that's what happened."

"What if Mr. Hadley stole them and hid them there?" Bob put in.

"Did the police have any suspicion of Mr. Hadley?" Jupiter asked.

Harry shook his head. "Mr. Hadley wouldn't do a thing like that. He liked us. And another thing, he was home the night the pictures were stolen."

"That seems to cover that," Jupiter admitted. "However, I can't help feeling it's all a little peculiar."

"What's peculiar?" Bob asked.

"We start out investigating a mysterious screaming clock, and we find it once belonged to a man who makes a hobby of naving all his clocks fixed so they scream. The investigation of the clock leads us to the mystery of who stole some valuable paintings and fixed it so Harry's father was sent to jail for the robbery. It seems peculiar one mystery should lead into another like that. Unless, of course, there's some connection between them."

"How could there be?" Pete asked.

"I haven't any idea," Jupiter admitted. "Still, Harry, I'd like to know anything you can tell us about Mr. Hadley. Bob, take notes."

What Harry could tell them wasn't really very much. Mr. Hadley, a short, plump, cheerful man, seemed to have plenty of money and they understood he had inherited it some years before. From observing the friends who dropped in to see him, Harry and his parents deduced Mr. Hadley had once been an actor. Many of them seemed to be theatrical people. However, Mr. Hadley never talked about his past.

He had testified at Harry's father's trial to say he believed Mr. Smith was innocent, and he had seemed very upset when Mr. Smith was convicted. Then, just after Harry's father had been sentenced to jail, Mr. Hadley had announced he was going abroad for his health. He asked Mrs. Smith to take care of the house while he was gone.

Mr. Hadley had left, taking two suitcases with him, and they hadn't heard a word from him since. Several friends had dropped by to see him, but eventually they all had stopped coming. After a time the money Mr. Hadley had left ran out, and just about then Mr. Jeeters had come by looking for a place to rent rooms. Mrs Smith had rented the top floor to him. He had made it clear that he wanted complete quiet and privacy, and he was very fussy about it.

"So that's it," Harry said. "That's all I know. It isn't much, you can see that. I suppose," he finished gloomily, "you can't really help my dad any. Nobody can. I apologize for acting nasty earlier. When you telephoned I made the hall clock scream to stop my mother from talking to you. I thought you were reporters or something. It's just—well, I feel so bad about everything."

"We understand," Jupiter said. "And we'll think about the problem. We'll let you know if we get any ideas."

They said good-bye to Harry, who climbed out of the car. Worthington started it up again.

"Where to, Master Jupiter?" he asked. "Home now?"

Jupiter deep in thought, shook his head.

"We started to drop in to see Alfred Hitchcock," he said. "If Mr. Hadley was an actor once, maybe Mr. Hitchcock knew him—he's worked with hundreds of actors. Take us to World Studios, Worthington."

"Very good, sir." The English chauffeur turned the car round and in a few minutes they were outside the front gate of World Studios, which occupied a whole block behind high walls. The gateman spoke on the phone, found that Mr. Hitchcock was in his office and would see them, and a few minutes later all three boys were seated opposite the famous director's big desk.

"Well, lads," Alfred Hitchcock rumbled, what brings you this way? Working on another investigation?"

"Yes, sir," Jupiter said. "Though it seems pretty mixed up right now and I'm not sure it means anything. You see, we started out to investigate a screaming clock and——"

"Screaming Clock!" Alfred Hitchcock interrupted in surprise. "What's happened to him, anyway? I haven't heard that name in years!"

7

The Clock is Stolen

"Him?" Jupiter exclaimed in amazement. "You mean there's a real person named Screaming Clock?"

"That was his nickname," Mr. Hitchcock explained. "His real name was Albert Clock, and for fun people called him Screaming Clock. You see, he was a screamer."

The more Mr. Hitchcock told them, the more puzzled the three became.

"A screamer?" Jupiter asked. "I'm not sure I know what that means."

"He screamed for a living," Mr. Hitchcock chuckled. "You see, back in the days before television, radio programmes featuring mystery stories were very popular. Why, at one time there were thirty-five mystery programmes a week on the radio. I don't believe there's even one on now. You lads are too young to remember, but those programmes were quite exciting.

"On a great many shows, someone screamed. A scream makes an exciting sound effect. You probably think any actor could scream if he had to, and of course that's true. But for a really exciting, professional scream the director hired a specialist. Someone like Albert Clock. I think he was the only full-time screamer in the business. I even used him in a couple of pictures.

"He was very versatile. He could sound like a child screaming, or a woman, or a man, or even various types of animals. He took pride in being expert in more different screams than anyone else alive. Of course radio dramas faded out of the picture when television became popular, and there's very little demand for a screamer any more. I used Bert Clock in one or two pictures some years ago, but after that he sort of vanished. That's why I said I hadn't heard of him in years. Did you say you're investigating him?"

"We didn't know it, but I guess we are," Jupiter said. "We started out to investigate a real clock."

He took the clock out of the bag and demonstrated it. Mr. Hitchcock was very much interested.

"A most unusual piece of work," he said. "I'd say Bert Clock had it constructed. After all, who would have a screaming clock made except a man whose nickname was Screaming Clock? It would appeal to him as a joke."

Jupiter told him about the roomful of clocks they had seen and heard. He also mentioned Mr.

Hadley, and Harry's father's arrest. Mr. Hitchcock looked thoughtful.

"Rather odd," he said. "This Hadley sounds like Bert Clock, all right. Clock was a small man, and you say Hadley was small and plump. He could easily have put on weight since I last saw him. Now that I think about it, I did hear he had come into money just about the time his radio work was becoming scarce.

"I can easily imagine him having a lot of different clocks made to scream the different screams he was an expert at. It would remind him of his past work and give his friends a chuckle. I can't imagine why he changed his name, though."

"Was he interested in art at all, Mr. Hitchcock?" Bob asked.

"Not that I know of. Some actors are collectors. In fact, here in Hollywood there is a surprising amount of valuable art owned by various actors, producers and directors. But I never heard of Bert Clock being interested in art."

"Thank you, sir." Jupiter stood up, and so did the others. "You've told us some things we'll have to think about. Mr. Clock also being Mr. Hadley is rather puzzling. And how the arrest of Harry's father fits in the picture I don't know yet. If we make any progress we'll let you know."

With that they said good-bye, and Worthington drove them back to Rocky Beach and The

Jones Salvage Yard. The chauffeur dropped them off, and the boys walked thoughtfully through the tall, iron gates into the crowded salvage yard. They were hardly inside when a man stepped out from behind a pile of lumber.

"You boys!" he said. "Remember me, do you?"

It was Mr. Jeeters, whom they had last seen an hour or so before at the home of Harry Smith.

"You have a clock," Mr. Jeeters growled. "In that bag. It belongs to me."

Unexpectedly he lunged at them, and snatched the zipper bag from Jupiter's hand.

"Now," he said, "it's my clock. I have it, and possession is nine-tenths of the law "

"You can't do that!" Pete shouted. He flung himself at Mr. Jeeters's legs in a flying tackle. Bob and Jupiter wouldn't let Pete attack unaided, and Jupe grabbed at the man's arm while Bob tried to pull the zipper bag from his hands.

Mr. Jeeters, however, was amazingly strong. He brushed Bob and Jupiter aside as if they were sparrows, then clamped powerful fingers on the back of Pete's shirt. He tossed him to one side in the dirt.

"Just try that again if you want to get hurt!" he sneered.

At that moment, Hans, one of the tall Bavarian yard helpers, put a large hand on the man's shoulder.

Pete flung himself at Mr. Jeeters's legs.

"I think better you give Jupe back his bag, Mister," Hans said.

"You big lug!" Mr. Jeeters snarled. "Let go of me!"

He aimed a fist at Hans's jaw. Hans ducked, and as the two men struggled wildly, Mr. Jeeters dropped the bag. Pete scooted in and recaptured it, then retreated to a safe distance as the two men, grunting and puffing, tried to throw each other down.

It was Hans who finally got the better of the struggle. Getting a grip around the other man's body, he lifted him high in the air like an angry child.

"What you want I do, Jupe?" Hans asked calmly. "Hold this fellow while you call police?"

"No, I don't believe so," Jupe answered, thinking swiftly. The police might not take the theft of an almost worthless alarm clock seriously. If they did, they'd probably want to hold on to the clock as evidence and now, more than ever, Jupe wanted to investigate the mystery behind it.

"Just put Mr. Jeeters down and let him go," Jupiter suggested. "We have the clock back."

"Okay," said Hans reluctantly, and he let the other man fall in a heap on the ground.

Mr. Jeeters picked himself up and brushed gravel from his clothes. "All right, you kids!" he growled. "You'll be sorry for this. You'll live

to regret the minute you ever saw that clock!"
And with those words, he stalked out.

8

Who is Rex?

"THE MEETING will come to order," Jupiter Jones
said, rapping on the desk. The other three boys
in the tiny office of Headquarters quieted. It was
the afternoon following their discovery of the
screaming clock and Mr. Jeeters's attempt to get
it away from them. They had been busy, and
now they were conferring to see what progress
they had made, if any.

Jupiter had phoned Harry Smith at his home
that morning. As Harry had recently got his
driver's licence and could drive the old car that
had belonged to his father, he had driven down
to The Jones Salvage Yard at Rocky Beach to
join them.

"Bob, give us your report," Jupiter said. Bob
had been the busiest of them all. That morning
he had driven into Los Angeles with his father,
who was a feature writer for a big Los Angeles
newspaper. His father had introduced him to the
man in charge of the records room, called "the

morgue" in newspaper slang. Here were hundreds of filing cabinets containing clippings of all the stories that had been in the newspaper, arranged both by subject matter and by name of the person involved.

Bob's job had been to look up first anything he could learn about Harry's father, Ralph Smith, and his trial, then about A. Clock or Mr. Hadley, then about thefts of valuable paintings in general.

Bob was armed with a sheaf of notes. He had a lot of information to pass on to the others, but he made it as brief as possible.

There wasn't much to tell about Ralph Smith's trial that they didn't know already. The evidence was circumstantial, but strong enough to convince the police that they had their man. They had tried to get Mr. Smith to admit he had been the art thief who had been operating around Hollywood and Los Angeles for some ten years, but Harry's father had stoutly maintained his innocence.

"Some of the thefts happened while you were still living in San Francisco, didn't they, Harry?" Bob asked.

"Yes, that's right. We only moved down to Hollywood about six years ago," Harry answered. "So you see, my dad has to be innocent. He couldn't have been involved in any of those first thefts."

"*If* the same ring was guilty all along, he couldn't," Jupiter put in. "Tell us about the series of art thefts in this city, Bob."

Bob obliged. There had been at least a dozen major robberies of valuable paintings in the last ten years, approximately at the rate of one a year. As Mr. Hitchcock had said, many wealthy film actors and directors collected art, and they had some immensely valuable paintings in their homes. Naturally, these weren't guarded as well as pictures in a museum would be. In every case the thieves had got in through a window or by picking the lock of a door, had cut the paintings out of their frames, and had vanished without leaving a trace.

"The police theory has been that these paintings were sold to wealthy South American collectors who would keep them hidden in their own private collections for their own enjoyment," Bob said. "Valuable paintings are known to just about everybody in the art world, so they couldn't have been sold legitimately. They must have been sold to people who wouldn't ever show them."

"And none of them were ever recovered?" Jupiter asked.

"None of them. Not until the three were found in Harry's house," Bob answered. He went on to tell them about the biggest theft, some two years before. Many rare paintings had been loaned to a gallery for a special exhibit. Before the exhibit even opened, the thieves had broken in and stolen five paintings, with a total value of half a million dollars.

"This wasn't a record, though," Bob added. "Not long ago someone cut out a door panel in an English museum and stole eight pictures valued at between four and eight million dollars. They were later recovered, but that's the record for an art theft so far."

"Wow!" exclaimed Pete. "That's a lot of money for paintings."

"Right," Bob agreed. "Anyway a lot of very valuable art has been stolen in this city, so smoothly that the police have been baffled every time. Apparently they now believe that Harry's father had a hand in most of the thefts, but they wouldn't even have suspected him if he hadn't been in the house trying to sell life insurance a few days before. So——"

"Now wait a minute!" Harry burst out angrily. "I tell you my father didn't do it. If you're trying to say that just because he sold insurance and got around to a lot of big houses——"

"Take it easy, Harry," Jupiter said quietly. "We don't believe your father did it. The question of how those pictures got under the linoleum in your kitchen is another mystery. We seem to have a lot of them. One: who stole the

51

pictures? Two: how did they get where they were found? Three: why did Mr. Hadley, or Mr. Clock, which seems to be his real name, go on a trip and disappear? Four: where did the clock actually come from, and what does it mean?"

He touched the clock, which stood on the desk in front of him.

"This clock certainly means something," he said. "Mr. Jeeters was mighty anxious to get it away from us yesterday. That means it has to be important somehow."

"I'm sorry I told Mr. Jeeters about you and the clock," Harry apologized. "But after you left he started asking me questions about you, and—well, he frightened my mother. So I told him you'd been there to ask about one of Mr Hadley's screaming clocks you had found, and that seemed to set him off. He grabbed your card away from me and left in a hurry."

"Fortunately, Hans was here to render us assistance," Jupiter said. "Tell me, Harry, has Mr. Jeeters acted suspiciously in any way while he's been living in the house?"

"He wanders round the house a lot at night!" Harry blurted out. "He claims he's a writer and can't sleep. One night I heard him tapping on walls like he was hunting for something."

"Mmmm." Jupiter pinched his lip and looked thoughtful. "I have an idea, but it may be all wrong. Let's get back to business. I don't see how we can solve the art thefts if the police can't. But we still have the mystery of the clock to investigate. We haven't puzzled out where it came from yet. Let's tackle that next."

"What good will that do my father?" Harry flared up. "He's in jail and you go around investigating an old clock!"

"We have to start someplace," Jupiter told him. "We have several mysteries here and I think the clock is a link between them somehow."

"Well, okay," Harry grumbled. "But how can you trace the clock if it was thrown out in someone's rubbish?"

"We have a message that was pasted on the bottom of it," Jupiter said. He opened a secret drawer in the desk, used for keeping small objects safe, and took out the paper they had found with the clock. He read the message out loud again:

Dear Rex:
Ask Imogene.
Ask Gerald.
Ask Martha.
Then act! The result will surprise even you.

"I still say, who are these characters?" Pete said. "How can we ever locate them and what do we ask them if we find them?"

"One thing at a time," Jupiter said. "It seems

the message is addressed to Rex. So I deduce that the clock containing the message must have been sent to this Rex. Let's locate Rex."

"As Pete says, how?" Bob put in.

"We must be logical," Jupiter said "Rex must be a friend of Mr. Clock, or Mr. Hadley—let's all call him Mr. Clock from now on for the sake of clarity. Anyway, Rex must be a friend to be addressed by his first name. Harry, did you bring Mr. Clock's address book?"

"I couldn't find one," Harry said, beginning to get interested. "But I did find a list of people he used to send Christmas cards to, stuffed in the back of a drawer."

He brought out a folded sheet of paper. Jupiter smoothed it out.

"Good," he said. "Mr. Clock's friends should be on a Christmas card list. There are about a hundred names here, and addresses too, all typed out. Now first let's find Rex."

"I see an Imogene, and two Geralds, and three Marthas," Bob said. "But no Rex."

"You're right, no Rex," Jupiter agreed.

"Wait a minute, wait a minute!" Bob burst out. "Look, there's a name, Walter King."

"What about it?" Pete asked.

"King in Latin is Rex," Bob said. "It might be a nickname for a man named King."

"It sounds more like a dog to me," Harry mumbled. But Jupiter was writing down the name of Walter King, and the address, on a card.

"Very good deduction, Bob," he said. "It's our only lead, so we'll have to try it. Now let's see about Imogene, Gerald, and Martha. Here's Miss Imogene Taylor, out in North Hollywood. Here are two Geralds, both over near Pasadena, and here are three Marthas, scattered around the city. There are four of us, so I propose we break up into two teams. Bob, you and Harry can be one team, as Harry has a car. Pete and I will be the other team and we'll call Mr. Gelbert at the Rent-'n-Ride Auto Agency for the car.

"We'll contact these people, see what we can learn, and get back here sometime this afternoon. Bob, you take Mr. King and Miss Imogene, since they both live in the same direction, and Pete and I will take the others."

"But what'll I ask them?" Bob inquired.

"Ask Mr. King if Mr. Clock sent him the clock, and whether he ever noticed the message on the bottom or did anything about it," Jupiter suggested. "Also why he threw it away. You'd better take the clock along with you, to show him in case he's forgotten."

"Right," Bob said. "What'll I say to Miss Imogene?"

"Well, you could ask her if Mr. Clock left any message with her," Jupe said. "Maybe you'll need to show her the clock to convince her the message is intended for you."

"All right, but suppose you need the clock to show to Gerald and Martha?"

"I'll take along a clock that looks like the original," Jupiter said. "Chances are we won't have to show it, just mention it. However, we have several old clocks around the salvage yard that look enough like Mr. Clock's.

"Well, is everything straight? If so, I suggest we get started. Bob and Harry, you two can go right away. Pete and I will have to wait for Worthington."

"Wait a minute!" Pete said suddenly. "Jupe, you're overlooking something very important. We can't start out now."

Jupiter blinked. "Why not?" he asked.

"Because," Pete told him with a straight face, "it's lunch-time."

9

Mystery Upon Mystery

"WE OUGHT TO BE NEARLY THERE," Bob said, scanning the street numbers as Harry drove his father's old sedan through an attractive section of North Hollywood. "Yes, there's Mr. King's number."

Harry parked the car and they both got out.

"Costs money to live out here," Harry remarked as they walked up the curving stone walk to the house.

Bob nodded. He carried in his hand the zipper bag containing the screaming clock. He wondered if they would find it had really come from this house whose bell he was now ringing.

The door opened and a woman looked out at them. She was not young, and she seemed to be under a strain.

"Yes, what is it?" she asked. "If you're collecting for the Boy Scouts, I already made a donation."

"No, ma'am" Bob said politely. "I wondered if I could speak to Mr. King, please."

"No you can't. He's ill. He's been in the hospital for several months."

"I'm very sorry to hear that," Bob said, thinking hard. If Mr. King was in the hospital, he couldn't very well have thrown away the clock. But he knew Jupe wouldn't give up without trying further, so he asked another question

"Is Mr. King's nickname Rex, ma'am?"

The woman stared at him. Bob was perfectly polite and looked respectable; otherwise she looked as if she would have closed the door in his face.

"Yes, it is," she said. "Why in the world are you asking? If this is some kind of game——"

"Oh, it isn't a game," Bob said hurriedly. "We're investigating a clock, Mrs. King. I'll show it to you." He took the clock from the zipper bag and held it up. "I wonder if you have ever seen it before."

"That horrible clock!" she cried. "Imagine sending such a thing to my husband, and when he was ill, too. If he'd ever heard it, it would have made him much worse. That dreadful scream!"

Bob and Harry exchanged quick glances. They had come to the right place, after all.

"Then Mr. Clock did send it to Mr. King?" Bob persisted.

"That horrible Bert Clock!" Mrs. King said indignantly. "Sending my husband a thing like that. Just because they used to work together years ago when my husband was writing a radio mystery show. Why, I plugged it in and set the alarm, never dreaming what it was, and when it went off that awful scream nearly gave me heart failure. I put it right into the rubbish and set it out for the refuse collector. Where on earth did you get it?"

"The refuse collector sold it to a friend of mine," Bob said. "Did you notice the message on the bottom?"

"Message on the bottom?" The woman frowned. "I didn't see any message. Of course, I got rid of the nasty thing the very next day.

There was a short letter with it from Bert Clock, but I threw it away."

"Can you possibly remember what it said?" Bob asked. "It's really very important."

"What it said? Oh, something about if my husband would listen to the clock and heed it well it might help mend his broken fortunes. Some nonsense. I think it was unpleasant of Bert Clock to play such a joke on my husband when he was ill and not working and worrying so much about the bills. They were very good friends once, too. I don't know why Bert Clock would want to scare us out of our wits with one of his horrible screams."

She paused, and frowned again.

"Why on earth do you want to know all this?" she asked. "Why are you interested in the clock?"

"We're trying to learn all about it," Bob said. "Mr. Clock has—well, he's disappeared and we think the clock may be a clue or something. You didn't notice where the clock was mailed from, did you?"

"No, I didn't. That's queer. Bert Clock disappeared. I wonder why—Oh, excuse me, I hear the telephone ringing. I've told you all I can, boys. Good-bye."

The door closed. Bob turned to Harry.

"See how an investigation works, Harry?" he said. "We've already learned a lot. I don't know what it all means, but even without Jupe I can tell that Mr. Clock sent this clock to Mr. King for a good reason. Only he never got it. He was sick in the hospital and his wife threw it away. Maybe Mr. King would have known what it meant, but we can't see him, so we'll have to figure it out for ourselves."

"Gosh!" Harry was getting into the spirit of the investigation. "Now let's try Miss Imogene Taylor. I wonder what she'll be able to tell us?"

As it turned out, Miss Taylor couldn't tell them much. She was a little, bird-like woman who lived in a tiny house out in Woodland Hills, a few miles beyond North Hollywood. It was a small cottage almost hidden behind bushes and banana trees, and Miss Taylor, with her grey hair and her chirping voice, and her old-fashioned gold spectacles, looked as if she had stepped out of a fairy tale.

She invited them into a living-room so full of papers and magazines and fancy cushions that it looked as if she could never find anything in it. But when she heard Bob's question about Mr. Clock and a message, she pushed her spectacles up on her forehead and started rummaging through her desk, talking all the time in little breathless chirps.

"My goodness!" she said. "Someone's really come. For the message. I thought it was just a joke. One of Bert Clock's jokes. He was a great practical joker in the studio. The radio stu.. that is. When we were all doing radio shows. I lost track of him after that. Until the letter came. With a piece of paper in it. The letter said to give the message to anyone who came asking for it, especially if they mentioned a clock. Now where on earth did I put my glasses? I can't see a thing without them."

Bob explained to her that she had pushed her glasses up on her forehead, and she quickly pulled them down. Her hand darted into a cubbyhole, and came out with a slip of paper.

"Here it is!" she said. "I knew I had it. Even if it's one of Bert's jokes, we were good friends, so I'll help it along. But surely you boys are too young to have heard Bert on the radio."

"Yes, ma'am," Bob said. "We never met him, but we're working on his joke, or whatever it is, to try to find out what he meant. Thank you very much for the message."

"Oh, you're welcome, you're welcome. Dear me, if you see Bert, give him my regards. Oh, what a wonderful screamer that man was. People used to stay up just to hear him on our radio show. It was called *A Scream at Midnight,* you know, and it was wonderfully scary. Rex King wrote it. He was wonderful at puzzles and clues and mysteries and things. My, yes. Can I give you boys a nice cup of tea? No? Well, if you have to go I understand. Boys are always in a hurry. That's the way boys are made."

Once outside in the car, Bob and Harry drew deep breaths.

"Whew!" Harry said and grinned. "I didn't think she'd ever stop talking. But anyway, we got a message. Let's see what it says."

Bob held the sealed envelope.

"Maybe we should wait for Jupe," he answered. "But—well, I guess we can take a look now."

He opened the envelope and slid out a slip of paper while Harry watched eagerly. Then their faces became puzzled. The message inside the envelope said:

It's quiet there even in a hurricane.
Just a word of advice, politely given.
Old English bowmen loved it.
Bigger than a raindrop; smaller than an ocean.
I'm 26. How old are you?
It sits on a shelf like a well-fed elf.

Bob and Harry stared at it in dismay.

"Good gosh!" Harry groaned. "What in the world does all that mean?"

10

Trouble for the Boys

THERE WERE three Marthas on Mr. Clock's list
of friends to receive Christmas cards, and they
all lived in the direction of Pasadena. Jupe and
Pete had to try two before they got the right one
—Mrs. Martha Harris, a plump widow who had
once been a radio and television actress but was
now retired.

Mrs. Harris kept cats—lots of cats, all Siamese.
They were all over the room as she talked to the
boys. A couple of them sat on the arms of her
chair, and she stroked them as she talked.

"Oh, my goodness, yes, I did know Bert
Clock!" she was saying. "How strange you
should come asking about him. No, it's not
strange, because I guess he expected someone to
come or he wouldn't have sent me the envelope
to give you."

"Mr. Clock sent you an envelope, ma'am?"
Jupiter said. "When was this?"

"Let me see now, about two weeks ago. In his
letter he said, 'If anyone comes asking for a mes-

Mrs. Harris kept cats—lots of cats, all Siamese.

sage from me, give him this envelope and my blessing. Let him have fun with it'."

She dug into a drawer, chasing a cat out of the way, and handed Jupiter an envelope.

"What in the world is Bert Clock up to these days?" she asked. "Last I heard, years ago, he'd come into a little money and retired. Anyway, there wasn't much work for a screamer after radio died."

"We don't know much about him," Jupiter answered. "He disappeared a few months ago."

"How mysterious!" exclaimed Mrs. Harris. "But then, Bert Clock was always a strange little fellow. Never could tell what he was thinking. Knew all sorts of odd people—jockeys and gamblers and people like that."

"Thank you very much for the envelope," Jupiter said. "Come on, Pete, we have to be going now."

They left Mrs. Harris with all her cats and went out to the car where Worthington was waiting.

"Now let's see this message," Pete said eagerly.

"Let's get in the car first," Jupiter said. They climbed into the rear of the car and Jupiter tore the envelope open. In it he found a sheet of paper similar to the one Bob and Harry had found, and a message that was even stranger because it wasn't in words, just numbers.

65

c

There was a whole column of numbers on the paper, and they started off like this:

3-27 4-36 5-19 48-12 7-11 15-9 101-2 5-16 45-37 98-98 20-135 84-9

They continued for another ten or fifteen lines, just as mysterious and meaningless.

"Jumping grasshoppers!" Pete exclaimed. "That means something?"

"It's obviously a code of some sort," Jupiter answered. "We'll get a message that makes sense once we solve the code. We'll tackle it later." Jupiter folded the message and put it into his pocket. "Now we must try to locate Gerald. There are two Geralds on the Christmas card list, and the closest one is Gerald Cramer We'll try him first."

He gave Worthington the address and they started off. Jupe pinched his lip thoughtfully as they drove, but said nothing, and Pete thought that if they were making any progress, he certainly wasn't aware of it. Still, maybe the next message would tell them more.

They pulled to a stop before a house in a rather run-down section. He and Pete got out and started up the walk.

"Of course, as there are two Geralds on the list," Jupiter remarked as they rang the bell, "our chance of getting the right one is only fifty-fifty. However——"

"Yeah? Whadda you want?"

A small man, not as tall as Jupiter, thin and bowlegged, appeared at the door.

"Excuse me," Jupiter said, ignoring the suspicious stare the small man gave him. "I believe you know Mr. Bert Clock?"

"Know Bert Clock? Who says I know Bert Clock?" the man demanded. "It's a lie. I never heard of Bert Clock in my life. Now beat it."

"One moment, Gerald, my friend," said a cultured voice, and a tall, distinguished-looking man with glossy black hair appeared behind the small man. He spoke with a Spanish accent.

"Why are you inquiring about someone known as Bert Clock?" he asked Pete and Jupiter. "You are not, I suppose, detectives?" And he smiled.

"As a matter of fact——" Pete started to say, but stopped when Jupiter nudged him.

"We are tracing a message Mr Clock left with some friends," Jupiter told the tall man. "He left it in different parts. One part he left with a friend named Gerald, and we thought that it might be Gerald Cramer, because his name is on Mr. Clock's Christmas card list."

"Very interesting," the man said. "Please come in. I believe I can help you. My friend here is Gerald Cramer and I apologize for his rudeness. He has had much trouble in his life."

Pete and Jupe followed the two men into a rather untidy living-room and sat down.

"I don't know what this is all about, Carlos," the small man grumbled. "But I don't like it."

"Please allow me to handle this matter," the man addressed as Carlos said sharply. To Jupiter he said, "You see, we are disturbed about Bert Clock's disappearance, and the curious message he sent to Gerald. We are anxious to know all you can tell us about him. Do you know where he is?"

"No, sir," Jupiter replied. "We're just tracing his message. You see, first we ran across a peculiar clock Mr. Clock sent someone, then——"

"A clock?" Carlos interrupted. "Do you have it there?" He looked fixedly at the small zipper bag Jupiter carried.

Jupiter took out the clock, which was an imitation of the real screaming one, and held it up.

"This is our credential, sir," he said.

The tall man took the clock and peered at it.

"A very ordinary looking clock," he said. "Now about the message. What was it?"

"It wasn't very clear," Jupiter answered. "It said to ask Martha and ask Gerald. But it didn't say what to ask them. We found a lady named Martha, who had received a letter from Mr. Clock and a sealed envelope she was to give to anyone asking about him. We came here next because Gerald Cramer was the next name on the Christmas card list. Does Mr. Cramer have a message for us?"

"He does indeed have a message," Carlos told him. "But it is a little different from the other. It says that before releasing it he must see the other message. May I see the message this lady named Martha gave you?"

"Well——" Jupiter hesitated. But Carlos was holding out his hand, and Jupiter reached in his pocket and brought out the paper with the long list of numbers on it. Carlos examined it, and his look was disappointed.

"Just numbers!" he said. "It seems to be a code. What does it mean?"

"I don't know," Jupiter said. "I hoped the next message would tell us. Gerald's message."

"Perhaps it will," Carlos agreed. "However, at this point I think I will take charge. This clock and these messages were never meant for you in the first place. Now just give me any other messages you may have and I will handle the matter henceforth."

"We haven't any other messages," Jupiter said, turning slightly pale, for Carlos suddenly looked menacing. "We'd like the clock back, please, and the message. It's our clock and our investigation——"

"Grab them, Jerry!" Carlos snapped. "We must search them and get any other messages they have."

"Gotcha, kid!" the little man grunted and wrapped strong, sinewy arms around Pete, pinning him tightly.

At the same moment, miles away, Bob and Harry also found themselves in trouble.

Leaving the home of Miss Taylor, Bob and Harry had started for Rocky Beach in Harry's car. They were only a mile or so from Rocky Beach, but still in the hills which form the Santa Monica Mountains, when Bob spotted a car behind them. It was dark blue with a white roof, and he had seen it earlier, when they first turned on to this little-used road. Now it was close, and coming up fast.

"Harry!" Bob said tensely. "I think we're being followed. That car's been behind us for miles. And now I think it's trying to catch up with us."

"We'll see about that!" Harry said and stepped hard on the gas.

The old car leaped forward, whipped around a curve, and started down a long hill.

Bob looked behind them. The blue car was closing the gap recklessly. It pulled up to within a hundred yards of them. Harry stepped harder on the gas. The old sedan was moving dangerously fast, but the blue and white car kept creeping closer.

Harry took a sharp turn so fast that the sedan

nearly went off the road at the edge of a cliff. When they straightened out, he turned a pale face to Bob.

"I'm not a good enough driver to go fast on these hills," Harry said to Bob. "He's going to catch us, whoever he is."

"Just a little farther," Bob said hopefully. "When we come to Rocky Beach, he'll be afraid to chase us."

"I'll try," Harry said. "I'll keep to the middle of the road—then he can't pass."

Doggedly he held the sedan in the middle of the road, and the car behind crept up almost to the rear bumper, looking back, Bob could see a figure hunched over the wheel. The man looked vaguely familiar, but he couldn't place him.

They roared along the lonely road, watching desperately for the descent from the hills to the city of Rocky Beach. Then, to avoid a hole in the road, Harry had to pull over close to the right shoulder. Immediately the pursuing car moved up beside them and began to edge them closer and closer to the side of the road.

"I've got to stop!" Harry yelled. "We'll be wrecked."

He stepped on the brake. As they slowed, the vehicle beside them slowed also. Bob peered across at it, trying to recognize the driver, who wore dark glasses. He couldn't place him, but still the sense of familiarity nagged at him.

Harry slowed the car to a stop. Their pursuer stopped beside them. Then, to their surprise, the blue car shot forward and disappeared around a curve.

"Now what do you make of that?" Harry asked in amazement. "First he chases us, then he beats it!"

An instant later they learned the reason. A siren wailed faintly in the distance, then it grew louder and louder, and a Rock Beach police car pulled up beside them. The siren died away as a grim-looking officer got out and walked towards them.

"All right, let's see your driver's licence!" he barked at Harry. "I've seen a lot of reckless driving, but none like you just did over these hills. Even if you have a licence, you're in for a lot of trouble!"

11

The Other Gerald

"I'VE GOT HIM!" the little man named Gerald yelled, his arms around Pete.

"Hold him!" ordered the bigger man, Carlos.

He snatched a letter-opener from the desk and pushed the point against Jupiter's chest.

"Now, young man, stand still and give me all the messages you have!"

Jupiter stood perfectly still. Pete, however, unable to see that Carlos had a weapon, was not giving up without a struggle. Being on the high school wrestling team, he knew something about breaking holds. He flung his arms outward while at the same time bending his body forwards with a whip-like motion.

Gerald went flying over his head. He crashed into Carlos, who went down with Gerald on top of him.

"Let's get out of here, Second!" Jupiter cried. Carlos, lying slightly stunned on the floor, still held the message they had obtained from Mrs. Harris. Jupiter reached down to pull it from his fingers, and turned towards the door. He and Pete bumped for a moment, sticking in the door, and then they were racing down the walk to the car.

"The clock!" Pete shouted. "You left the clock!"

"It wasn't the real clock anyway," Jupiter replied as they got in the car. "Worthington, get us away from here fast!"

"Very good, sir," the chauffeur said. He had the car moving so quickly that Jupe and Pete tumbled on to the floor in the rear. In a moment they got untangled and sat up. Jupe held up the message.

"This is the important thing, the message from Mr. Clock," he said. "I got it back and we——"

He stopped. They both looked at the paper.

It was torn across the middle. Jupiter only had half of it. The other half was still back in Carlos's hand.

"Oh, oh!" Pete said. "That's bad. We've lost half the message."

"Maybe we ought to go back," Jupiter said thoughtfully.

"And tackle those guys again?" Pete protested.

"No," Jupiter agreed after another moment of thought. "By now Carlos would have the other half of the message hidden and would deny everything."

"Where to now, sirs?" Worthington asked from up front. "Or do you wish to return to Headquarters?"

"No," Jupiter answered. "We still have one more message to find. Gerald Cramer was the wrong Gerald, obviously. We'll try Gerald Watson next." He gave Worthington the address, and he and Pete settled back.

"Listen, First," Pete said, "I've been thinking. That little guy, Gerald Cramer, didn't have any message from Mr. Clock. Just the same he and

Carlos were awfully interested as soon as they learned about the messages. What do you make of that?"

"I'm not sure," Jupiter answered. "It suggests to me they know something about Mr. Clock that we don't, and consider the messages important. We'll just have to try to find out why Maybe the messages themselves will tell us when we solve them."

"When we solve them!" Pete laughed hollowly. "By then we'll be old men with long white beards, if that message you've got is any sample. Besides, you only have half of it."

"I'm aware of that," Jupiter snapped. "We'll just have to do the best we can. Worthington, is this the address?"

"It appears to be, sir," the English chauffeur said as he brought the car to a stop. "Do you anticipate any danger this time?"

"I don't think so," Jupiter replied. "If we need you, we'll shout. Come on, Second."

Pete followed him up the walk to a nice little Spanish-style house surrounded by gardens. An elderly man was pottering with some roses in front, and he looked up.

"Mr. Gerald Watson?" Jupiter asked.

The man nodded. "That's me," he said, taking off his gardening gloves. "What can I do for you? I don't suppose you want my autograph?" He chuckled. "It's been years since anyone wanted my autograph. But when I starred as the detective in *A Scream at Midnight*, a lot of people used to want it. I don't suppose you ever heard it, though, did you?"

"No, sir," Jupiter agreed. "It was a spooky radio show, wasn't it?"

"The spookiest," Gerald Watson said. "Used to open with a scream—Bert Clock did the screaming—and then went on to all kinds of weird mysteries. Bert and Rex King wrote it. I believe Bert suggested the plots and Rex wrote them. He was very good at puzzles and clues and so on. Well, well, that's ancient history.

"What are you here for, anyway, boys? Not selling magazine subscriptions, I hope?"

"We've come for a message that Mr. Clock sent you," Jupiter said. "He left another message saying to ask you for it."

"Oh, the message!" Mr. Watson quickly brightened up. "Yes, yes, of course. Out of the blue it came—haven't heard from Bert Clock in years, except for Christmas cards. Come in, come in. I'm sure I can dig up that message for you."

He led them into the house, into a neat and tidy room whose main feature was a big tape recorder and a shelf that held box after box of recorded tapes. From a desk drawer he drew an envelope. It had been opened.

"Here you are," Mr. Gerald Watson said. "I

opened it—curiosity got too strong for me. But I couldn't understand a word of it."

Jupiter took out the message and he and Pete examined it. It said:

Take one lily; kill my friend Eli.
Positively number one.
Take a broom and swat a bee.
What you do with clothes, almost.
Not Mother, not Sister, not Brother; but perhaps Father.
Hymns? Hams? Homes? Almost, not quite.

"Isn't that a dandy message?" Mr. Watson asked as they read it. "I tried to figure out what it means, but I didn't get anywhere. That first line—I never knew any friend of Bert's named Eli. Sounds as if he meant to kill Eli and put a lily on his chest, doesn't it?" He chuckled. " 'Give it to anyone who comes asking for a message,' he said, and you did, and I have, so there it is. By the way, I don't think I know who you are."

"Oh, excuse me, here's our card." Jupiter gave him a Three Investigators business card. Mr. Watson studied it gravely, then shook their hands.

"Delighted to meet you," he said. "If you're interested in Bert Clock, perhaps you'd like to hear some of the old radio shows we did to-

Bob and Harry stood in front of Police Chief Reynolds's desk.

gether—the ones that started with him screaming. They were jim-dandies! Every time he screamed differently. And the plots! They don't write shows like that for television these days. All those boxes of tape you see—they hold every show I did with Bert Clock."

Pete and Jupiter were tempted. They knew that some of the old radio shows had been much spookier than anything on television now. But they really couldn't spare the time. So they said good-bye and went out to the waiting car, still puzzling over the message. Jupiter asked Worthington to take them back to The Jones Salvage Yard, and said to Pete, "I hope Bob and Harry will be there when we get back. If they managed to get a message, too, we'll put them all together and see if we can puzzle them out."

Bob and Harry, however, were not at Headquarters—at least not Headquarters for The Three Investigators. They were at the Rocky Beach police headquarters, being led into Chief Reynolds's office by the policeman who had arrested Harry for speeding.

"The chief says he knows you," the officer said to Bob. "But don't think you'll get away with anything. You speed-happy kids are a menace to decent citizens!"

He led them into an office where Chief Reynolds, a heavy-set man, sat behind a big desk covered with papers. The chief looked up.

"Well, Bob," he said, "I'm sorry to see you here. What Officer Zebert tells me sounds rather serious. Driving recklessly over the mountains could have killed both of you and maybe other people, too."

"Excuse me, Chief," Bob said. "We weren't driving recklessly. We were being chased by another car. It had just caught us when Officer Zebert came up, and the other driver got away."

"Being chased, eh?" The officer smiled knowingly. "You should have seen them going round those curves, Chief! Then they were racing side by side down Mountain Road. If anyone else had come along then, they would have all been killed."

"Now why should another car chase you?" Chief Reynolds asked. "Anyone could guess you wouldn't be carrying much money with you."

"We're on a case," Bob said. "We're investigating a mysterious clock."

"A mysterious clock!" It was Officer Zebert who spoke. "Did you ever hear such a crazy story, Chief?"

"It's true," Bob insisted doggedly. "We investigated a green ghost* once, Chief. You remember that time. You even asked us—that is, Jupiter Jones and Pete Crenshaw and me—to help you find out what it was."

* The Mystery of the Green Ghost

He was referring to a mystery which Chief Reynolds at the time had frankly admitted had him totally baffled. Now the chief nodded.

"That's true," he said. "Where is this clock and what's so mysterious about it?"

"It's in the car out back," Bob said. "If we could bring it in, we could show you why it's so queer."

"Right!" the chief said. "Zebert, go bring the clock here."

"It's in a zipper bag on the front seat," Bob said, as the officer departed.

"You know I want to believe you, Bob," the chief said as they waited. "But we've had so much speeding and reckless driving by teenagers that we have to do something about it—Here comes Officer Zebert. Did you find the clock, Zebert?"

The officer shook his head.

"Nothing there," he said. "The front seat's empty. No clock, No bag. Nothing."

Bob and Harry stared at each other.

"Golly!" Bob exclaimed. "The clock's been stolen!"

12

Questions—But No Answers

"I WONDER what's keeping Bob and Harry?"
Pete said as Jupiter, at his desk in Headquarters,
bent over the message from Mr. Watson. "I'll
take a look outside and see if they're coming
yet."

He went to the corner, where a length of thin
stovepipe came down from the roof. From this
Jupiter had fashioned a periscope which he
called the See-All. Junk was piled as high as the
roof around the trailer, hiding it from the outside world, and it was necessary to use the See-
All to see over it.

Pete took a quick look and reported that
Harry's car had just driven into the yard. A few
moments later a code rap came on the trapdoor
which opened into Tunnel Two. Pete lifted the
trapdoor and Bob and Harry, looking rather
tired, climbed into the office.

"Did you get the message?" asked Jupiter.

"We got a message, yes," Bob said. "But we
can't understand it."

"May I see it?" Jupiter requested. "And do you have the clock?"

"Well, no, I don't have it." Bob looked unhappy.

Jupiter glanced at him sharply. "You've lost the clock?"

"It was stolen!" Harry blurted out. "While the car was parked at the police station."

"What were you doing at the police station?" Pete asked. "Did you run into something too big to handle?"

"We were arrested for speeding," Harry reported. "You see, coming over the hills someone started chasing us——"

Between them he and Bob told the story of their adventure. Bob finished up by saying, "Chief Reynolds finally let us go. He said he didn't know what we were mixing into, but if it was something important enough to be chased for, we'd better turn it over to the police."

"I don't think the police would really be interested in what we know so far," Jupiter said. "They would be inclined to call it some kind of joke. We ran into a little trouble, too."

He and Pete told of their encounter with Carlos and the little man, who, Jupiter now said, looked like a jockey or an ex-jockey.

"So you see," he said, "someone's interested in the clock and the messages. The clock was probably stolen by the same man who chased you two. When he saw the officer taking you to police headquarters, he followed and took the clock from the car."

"But who would know about the clock and the messages?" Bob demanded. "That's what I don't see."

"Well, we know Mr. Jeeters knows about the clock," Jupiter said. "And he may have told someone else. And then there are Carlos and Gerald Cramer. We obligingly told them almost everything before we learned it was the wrong Gerald. So several people know quite a bit about our activities."

"Too much to suit me!" Pete grumbled. "Is that message Bob got as wild as the ones we have, Jupe?"

Jupe spread out the message Bob had handed him.

"It is equally incomprehensible," he said.

"Can't you just say it's a skullbuster?" Pete groaned. "Why be a walking dictionary?"

"All right," Jupiter agreed, with a slight grin. "It's a ring-tailed, double-barrelled skullbuster. Is that better?"

"Now you're talking my language!" Pete said.

"Now let's see if we can make any sense out of it," Jupiter went on. "First, Bob, give me a full report on your meeting with Mr. King and with Miss Imogene Taylor."

Bob did so, and Jupe listened carefully, making mental notes.

"So Mr. King is sick in the hospital," he murmured. "And Mr. Clock sent the clock to him thinking he would investigate and get all these messages and solve them—and then what? That's the question."

"The message pasted to the bottom of the clock said, 'Then act. You'll be glad you did'," Bob reminded him.

"Exactly," Jupiter said. "But why would he be glad? What would happen? It's up to us to find out. Now let's take the messages in order. The message Bob and Harry got from Miss Taylor is obviously first, so let's study it first."

He spread out the message and they all stared at it. It still said:

It's quiet there even in a hurricane.
Just a word of advice, politely given.
Old English bowmen loved it.
Bigger than a raindrop; smaller than an ocean
I'm 26. How old are you?
It sits on a shelf like a well-fed elf.

"I still don't see how that can be a message," Harry said. "Unless it's a code of some kind."

"It was intended for this Mr. King, who's sick," Jupiter reminded them. "He's very good at clues and puzzles. This was something for him to puzzle out. If he could do it, so can we."

"Speak for yourself," Pete said gloomily.

"At first glance," Jupe went on, "these peculiar sentences look something like the definitions of words in a crossword puzzle. My deduction is that each line means one word, and when we get all the words, we'll have a message six words long."

"But what words?" Pete wanted to know. "Where is it quiet even in a hurricane?"

"The best place to be in a hurricane is in a storm cellar," Harry said.

"Or a bank vault," Bob added.

"I don't know." Jupiter pinched his lip. "Maybe a bank vault would fit. We're probably talking about something valuable, you know"

"How do you figure that?" Pete demanded.

"Why go to so much trouble unless it's about something valuable?" Jupiter asked. "No, it's about something valuable and it could be in a bank vault. Now let's go on to line two. It says, *'Just a word of advice, politely given.'* Now, what other words are there for 'advice'? Pete, hand me that dictionary on the shelf."

Pete handed him the dictionary from a shelf of books, and Jupiter leafed through it.

"Here we are," he said, " 'Advice: an opinion or recommendation to a course of action.' Let's see how that fits. Bank vault—opinion— . . . It doesn't sound right."

"It sure doesn't," Pete agreed. "If you want my suggestion——"

"Pete, stop!" Jupiter cried.

Pete stared at him. "Stop? Why? I was just going to tell you my suggestion——"

"That's it!" Jupiter told him. "Suggestion. A suggestion would be a polite way to give advice, wouldn't it? I think you've solved the line for us."

Pete blinked. "Then maybe it isn't so hard after all," he said. "Still, I don't make any sense out of 'bank vault—suggestion'."

"Neither do I," Jupiter agreed. "But we still have to get the rest of the words."

"The third line is, *'Old English Bowmen loved it,'*," Bob said. "But loved what? Bowmen were archers, they shot bows and arrows, so maybe they loved arrows."

"Arrows are plural, not singular," Jupe said. "Bowmen are also supposed to have loved a good battle."

"Bank vault—suggestion—battle!" Harry exclaimed. "That's worse than ever."

"I agree," Jupiter said, frowning. "But——" At that moment his aunt's voice came in through the open skylight.

"Jupiter! Dinner-time. We're closing up shop."

"I'll be right there, Aunt Mathilda," Jupiter said into a microphone that connected with a speaker in his aunt's office. To the others he said:

"I guess we'll have to quit for the day. Harry, can you come back to-morrow?"

"I don't think so," Harry told him. "My mother needs me to help her round the house. Besides, I can't see that we're getting anywhere."

"Well, then we'll keep in touch with you," Jupiter answered. "You can keep an eye on Mr. Jeeters. Don't forget how Mr. Jeeters tried to get that clock from us. Maybe he was the one who followed you and Bob and stole the clock from the parked car."

"I'll keep an eye on him," Harry agreed. "I don't trust him. He's up to something."

"Meanwhile we three——" Jupiter began. He was interrupted again, this time by the ringing of the telephone. He picked it up.

"Three Investigators, Jupiter Jones speaking," he said.

"Hello," said a voice he couldn't place at first. "This is Gerald Watson. You called at my home this afternoon for a message from Bert Clock."

"Yes, sir?" Jupiter answered.

"Well, I've been thinking it over and I just thought I ought to tell you—since you left me your card—about what happened after you left."

"Something happened?" Jupiter asked.

"Someone else came asking for the message,"

Mr. Watson told him. "A tall, dark-haired South American with a small friend. They said Bert Clock had sent them."

"But you couldn't give them the message," Jupiter said, puzzled. "You'd already given it to us."

"That's true," Mr. Watson said. "But they asked whom I had given it to and I showed them your card. They copied down your names. I began to wonder whether I had done the right thing. I didn't like them very much—that Carlos was too smooth a talker."

"It can't be helped," Jupiter said. "Thank you for letting me know, Mr. Watson."

He hung up and turned to the others.

"Carlos and Gerald Cramer know our names now," he said. "They undoubtedly want the messages and the clock. Mr. Jeeters wanted the clock. Some unknown person, maybe a third party we haven't met yet, actually stole the clock. There's an awful lot of interest in this mystery, and I wish I knew just what we're in the middle of."

13

Bob Finds More Clues

THE NEXT MORNING Bob was hurrying through breakfast to get to The Jones Salvage Yard when the telephone rang. It was Miss Bennett, the local librarian, asking if he could come in and spend half a day or perhaps more helping out. Bob had a part-time job at the library, helping mend damaged books, replacing books on the shelves, and other odd jobs.

He couldn't very well say no, though he hated to have Jupiter and Pete working on the mysterious messages without him. He told Miss Bennett he'd be there in twenty minutes, and set off on his bicycle.

Miss Bennett greeted him with relief, for her assistant was away that day. Bob plunged into work and was kept busy until lunch-time. Miss Bennett wanted him to stay for part of the afternoon, too, and Bob agreed. He quickly ate the sandwiches his mother had made so he could spend a few minutes doing some research.

On a hunch he decided to read up about hurricanes, for a hurricane was mentioned in the first mysterious message. He read a long article in the encyclopedia, and came across a fact which made him jump slightly with excitement. He wrote it down, and then checked up on archery, especially old English bowmen. Again he came on a fact that filled him with suppressed excitement. Next he tried oceans. Nothing that looked useful came to his attention, and lunch hour was over so he went back to work, anxious to get to the salvage yard and tell Jupe and Pete what he had learned.

However, Miss Bennett needed him all the rest of the day, and it was not until five in the afternoon that she finally thanked him and said that he could go. Bob streaked away on his bicycle and rode quickly to the salvage yard. He found Jupiter and Pete unhappily at work stacking second-hand merchandise in neat rows at the back of the cabin which served as an office.

"We've been working all day," Jupiter explained as Bob got off his bike. "Uncle Titus brought in a truckload of stuff this morning, and Aunt Mathilda has had us sorting it out ever since. Hans and Konrad are off to-day. So we haven't made any progress on our investigation."

"Did you hear from Harry at all?" Bob asked.

"Just a phone call. Mr. Jeeters cornered him and asked him what he did with us yesterday.

He scared Harry. Harry told him we'd got some crazy messages that didn't mean anything. He also told him about someone stealing the screaming clock. That seemed to make Mr. Jeeters very angry."

"Mr. Jeeters knows something we don't," Bob said. "If we ever solve those messages maybe we'll find out what it is. Listen, Jupe, I learned——"

"Jupiter!" rang out Mrs. Jones's voice. "Step lively there! You haven't finished yet. Bob Andrews! I'm glad you're here. You can start listing all this stuff Titus bought. Make a nice neat job of it. I'll go in and get dinner."

She came over and shoved a big notebook into Bob's hands. It was a record of merchandise that had been added to the stock of The Jones Salvage Yard.

"Keep a careful account now, Bob," she said. "And I expect everything nice and neat before you boys stop. I'll call you when dinner is ready."

With that she left, and Bob began working again. Pete and Jupe stacked the newly acquired items and called them out.

"One rocking chair!" said Pete.

"One rocking chair." Bob wrote it down.

"One set of garden tools, rusty," called Jupe.

"One set garden tools, rusty," wrote Bob.

So it went on for nearly an hour. When they

had finally got everything in order, Pete and Jupiter flung themselves down, exhausted. Bob was a bit tired, too, but anxious to see how his research would help solve the messages.

"Listen," he said, "aren't we going to work on those messages?"

"I'm too tired to think," Pete moaned. "I'm too tired to move. Just go away and leave us alone, Bob. I don't even want to think about mysteries now."

"I can't think clearly either," Jupe admitted. "We'd better wait until to-morrow, Bob."

"But I have some clues!" Bob said. "Two of them. I think they'll fit."

"What's a clue?" Pete groaned. "I never heard the word."

"We can at least listen to what Bob has to tell us," Jupiter said. "All right, Bob, what have you learned?"

"Well," Bob said, "while I was at the library to-day I looked up hurricanes. And there's one quiet spot in a hurricane—the very centre of it. Away from the centre the wind may be blowing at a hundred miles an hour, but in the centre it can be perfectly calm, with the sun shining."

"Go on, Bob!" Jupiter said.

"The centre of a hurricane is called the eye!" Bob said triumphantly. "Get it? Eye is pronounced the same as the pronoun I! I'll bet that's the first word of the message."

The Three Investigators tried to decipher the message.

"The only message I want to hear is 'Dinner's ready'," Pete grumbled.

"I think Bob has hit on something," Jupiter said, rousing himself. "What's your other clue, Bob?"

"I also looked up archery and old English bowmen," Bob continued. "They used to use wood from the yew tree a lot in making their bows. So if we said that old English bowmen loved yew, we have another word. Y-e-w is pronounced exactly the same as y-o-u."

"Bob, I think you're right," Jupiter said, after a pause for reflecting. "Before Aunt Mathilda calls us to dinner, let's go into Headquarters and have another try at that message."

"Can't it wait until to-morrow?" Pete asked. But he got up and followed when Bob and Jupiter started towards Tunnel Two.

Five minutes later they were grouped round the desk with the first mysterious message spread out before them.

"The first line of the message says, *'It's quiet here even in a hurricane'*," Jupiter read. "If Bob's right, the word that is meant is 'eye'." He wrote it down. "Now we already think that the line, *'Just a word of advice, politely given'* means 'suggestion'." He wrote that down, too. "So if the line, *'Old English bowmen loved it'* means 'yew', we have our first three words Like this."

He wrote: *Eye suggestion yew.*

"That looks a little funny," he added, "but it makes perfectly good sense if we change the wording a little, and get *I suggest you*."

"I suggest you," Pete exclaimed, forgetting his weariness. "That does start out like a sensible message after all. Okay, Jupe, what's the fourth word?"

"The clue is, *'Bigger than a raindrop; smaller than an ocean'*," Jupiter said. "Meaning some body of water smaller than an ocean. That could be a river, a pond, a lake or a sea."

"Sea!" exclaimed Bob. "Meaning s-e-e. That must be it. Now we come to the fifth clue, *'I'm 26. How old are you?'* That's tougher. What's 26 years old?"

"The suggestion of age is an attempt to mislead us." Jupe decided. "I'm sure that number 26 here means something that is twenty-sixth in a series of things. The most common thing that comes to mind as being number 26 is——"

"Let me try!" Pete spoke up. "There are 26 letters in the alphabet. Number 26 is the letter Z. Does that fit?"

"It does if we just use the sound of it," Jupiter told him. "Z sounds like 'the.' And 'the' fits into the message. Now we just need the last clue, *'It sits on a shelf like a well-fed elf.'* Any ideas, either of you?"

"I looked up elves at the library but I didn't find anything," Bob confessed.

"What sits on a shelf?" Pete asked. "Like an elf?"

"The word elf is just another word to confuse us," Jupiter said. "Bob, you spent the whole day looking at shelves. Didn't it occur to you what sat on them?"

"Books!" Bob yelled. "And every one of them full of words. You could say they were well-fed —with words."

"I'm sure we have the message now," Jupiter said. "I'll write it out." He did, and got:

I suggest you see the book.

"Wow, we did it!" Pete cried. "But what does it mean? What book are we supposed to see? And when we see it, what do we do with it?"

"There are two more messages to be solved," Jupiter said. "When we——"

He was interrupted by Mathilda Jones's voice.

"Boys! Dinner! Come and get it!"

"I guess that means we have to stop now," Jupiter said reluctantly. "We'll try again to-morrow when we're fresh. We'll make better progress then, anyway."

So, leaving the mysterious messages for further work the next day, they went hungrily in to dinner.

D

14

A Call for Help

DURING DINNER the boys discussed the meaning of the message they had just unravelled. It suggested they see a book. But what book? They had no idea.

"Could it mean the Bible?" Pete ventured. "That's known as the Good Book by a lot of people."

"I don't think so," Jupiter said, taking a second helping of dessert. "Though it might. Maybe the next message will tell us more."

"What project are you boys working on now?" Titus Jones asked from the head of the table.

"We have some mysterious messages to decipher, Uncle Titus," Jupiter said. "So far we've just made a beginning."

"You boys and that club of yours!" Mathilda Jones exclaimed, cutting another piece of cake for Pete. "I declare it's a good thing I give you some work to do and keep you out in the open air or you'd spend all your time working puzzles."

As the boys had once had a puzzle-solving club, which had later become The Three Investigators, Mrs. Jones had it firmly in her mind that their chief activity was still solving puzzles.

"Well, I'm not solving anything more tonight," Jupiter said with a yawn. "You kept us out in the open air all day, Aunt Mathilda, and I'm going to bed early."

"I'll buy a double helping of that," Pete agreed, and he yawned, too. "It was a great dinner, Mrs. Jones, but if you'll excuse me, I think I'll ride home now and turn in."

Pete and Bob both said good night and departed. After riding together for a block or two, they separated to go to their own homes.

Neither of them noticed a small delivery van which followed them slowly and when they separated, continued to follow Bob.

Jupiter meanwhile was helping his aunt clear the table. However, he yawned constantly.

"Heavens to Betsy," his aunt exclaimed. "You must really be tired, Jupiter. You go on up to bed. Scoot, now."

Jupiter went gladly and tumbled into bed. But as soon as he was in bed, he started wondering about the other mysterious messages.

I suggest you see the book. That was the first message. What book? Did the second message tell? He tried to remember the second message. The harder he tried to remember, the wider awake he became. Sleep got further and further away. At last he came to a decision. He would have to try to solve the second message before he could get any sleep.

He got dressed again and went downstairs. His aunt and uncle were watching television, and they looked up in surprise.

"Mercy and goodness, Jupiter!" his aunt said. "I thought you were asleep."

"I started thinking about something," Jupiter said. "A—well, a sort of puzzle. I left it out in the salvage yard. I'm going to go get it and have a last look at it before I go to sleep."

"I certainly do hope you don't wear out your brains with all these puzzles," Mrs. Jones sighed.

Jupiter crossed the short distance to the front entrance of the salvage yard. The gates were padlocked; however, he had his own entrance which he used when necessary. He walked along the gaily painted fence until he came to two boards painted green.

Jupiter pushed his finger against a special spot, and the two boards swung silently back, revealing a narrow entrance. This was Green Gate One, one of several secret entrances and exits to the yard known only to The Three Investigators. Jupiter squeezed through and found himself in the special workshop section.

He now proceeded to the printing press, found the piece of iron grillwork at the back, and moved it, revealing the entrance to Tunnel Two. He scrambled through Tunnel Two, pushed up the trapdoor, and entered the office.

He had left the secret messages in a drawer of the desk. Switching on the overhead light, he got them out. The first message, the one that said *I suggest you see the book,* he put off to one side. The second message, which he and Pete had obtained from Gerald Watson, he spread out in front of him.

On the face of it, it was very mystifying. The six lines of the message said:

Take one lily; kill my friend Eli.
Positively number one.
Take a broom and swat a bee.
What do you do with clothes, almost.
Not Mother, not Sister, not Brother; but perhaps Father.
Hymns? Hams? Homes? Almost, not quite.

However, after he had read it a couple of times, Jupiter began to get some ideas. Solving the first message had shown him the right way to proceed. Each line was a clue to a word, rather like the clues in crossword puzzles.

The first line said to take *one lily.* He did this by writing the words down on a sheet of paper, so that he had: ONE LILY. He stared at it for a moment. Where did Eli come in? Then he saw it. The three middle letters of the two words spelled ELI!

Triumphantly Jupiter rubbed out the three letters, thereby "killing" Eli. What he had left was ONLY.

"Only!" Jupiter exclaimed to himself. "That's it! Now the second line says, *'Positively number one.'* In the first message, number twenty-six stood for the letter Z. Suppose number one stands for *A*? That fits fine. The message starts *'Only a—'.*"

Without even stopping, he wrote down BROOM, from the third sentence, and erased the *B*, for the line said, *'Take a broom and swat a bee.''* What was left was the word ROOM.

Jupiter now working with increasing excitement, talking to himself as he sometimes did when working alone.

"*'What you do with clothes, almost.'* Well, what do you do with clothes? You wear them, naturally. What word is almost 'wear' but not quite? How about 'where'? That has to be it. Now the message is, *'Only a room where—'.* That makes sense so far."

He wrote it down, and then tackled the fifth line.

This gave him more trouble. He tried different words for father, such as "Dad," "Pop," "head of the family." But none of them made any sense.

102

He stopped and pinched his lip. Suppose the word father was meant to suggest something more. Father Christmas? No, that didn't seem to fit. Father Time? This whole business was about clocks, so that must be it. *Father Time!*

Now he dashed off the last line. What sounds almost, but not quite, like hymns, hams, and homes? There were only two likely words, hems and hums. Hems didn't fit. Hums did. With a feeling of triumph he wrote down *Only a room where Father Time hums*.

But time doesn't hum. It just passes by silently. Or if you mean a clock, it ticks by, unless——

"That's it!" Jupe exclaimed to himself. "All those clocks in Mr. Clock's study are electric, and they all hum. That's a room where time really hums."

Now he had two complete messages.

I suggest you see the book.
Only a room where Father Time hums.

The room had to be the room in Mr. Clock's house where all the screaming clocks were. He had no idea which book was meant. However, he might get some clue to that later. Now he took out the torn sheet of paper which contained the first part of the message they had obtained from Mrs. Martha Harris.

Jupiter studied the first line of numbers.
3-27 4-36 5-19 48-12 7-11 15-9

Ordinarily they wouldn't have meant anything at all to him. But since the messages he had already solved mentioned a book, he thought he understood. A very popular type of code message involves using a book. The sender of the message picks out words in the book which fit the message, then writes down just the page and the word number, and sends only the numbers to the receiver. The receiver of the message has a copy of the same book, and by looking up the page and word number he can easily read the message. These numbers almost surely referred to pages and words in some book.

Only Jupe didn't have a copy of the book, didn't know what book it was, and in any case only had half the page and word numbers!

But he had done enough for one night. He put the messages back in the desk and was about to let himself down into Tunnel Two when the phone rang. Surprised, he picked it up.

"Three Investigators, Jupiter Jones speaking," he said.

"Jupe!" It was Bob's voice and he sounded scared. "Jupe, I'm in a bad jam. I need help!"

15

Bob in a Jam

RIDING HOME by himself, Bob did not notice the small van that was following him. But as they came to a block where there were no houses, it speeded up and passed him. It came to a stop and a boy jumped out.

"Bob!" he called.

Bob put on his brakes in surprise. It was Harry, and he looked very upset. Bob jumped off his bicycle and walked it up to Harry.

"What is it, Harry? Something wrong?"

The rear door of the van opened and a small wiry man jumped out.

"There'll be plenty wrong unless you obey orders," he growled. "Don't try to make a break for it."

"I'm sorry, Bob!" Harry's face twisted with unhappiness. "They made me stop you. They've got Mom locked up back at the house."

"Never mind the long explanations," the man snapped. "Just give me your bicycle and climb into the van. Move, now!"

Bob looked around quickly. There was no one on the street to call to for help. And it wouldn't be any use running—he couldn't run fast enough to get away.

The man grabbed his bicycle and gave him an impatient shove.

"Get into the van!" he said. "You, Harry, get in with him."

Bob climbed up into the dark van and Harry followed. The man pushed the bicycle in after them. The rear door slammed and locked They were prisoners in the van.

"They swore they wouldn't hurt us, Bob," Harry said in a low voice. "All they want is information. About the messages and the clock. I couldn't tell them enough so they came to get it from one of you. They've been watching the salvage yard for a chance to grab one of you alone."

"But who are they?" Bob asked as the van rocked along towards some unknown destination.

"Mr. Jeeters is one of them. There are two others. One is a tall man named Carlos, and the other is the little man you saw. His name is Jerry. He used to be a jockey."

"Carlos and Gerald!" Bob exclaimed. "They're the two Pete and Jupiter saw yesterday afternoon, the ones who got part of one message from them."

106

"Yes, and that's stirred them up. They want to know what the message means," Harry said unhappily. "They're looking for something valuable and they're determined to find it. They think we have the clue to where it's hidden."

"If we do we don't know it," Bob said "Jupe said, though, that he was sure something valuable was involved."

"Carlos and Jerry came to see Mr. Jeeters this afternoon. They had a long talk. Then they grabbed hold of me and made me tell them everything I knew. Gee, I'm sorry, Bob, but I had to. They're tough. They said that if I didn't co-operate in everything they wanted, my mother would suffer for it."

"You had to do it," Bob said. "Don't blame yourself. You say they've got your mom locked up?"

"Yes, back at Mr. Hadley's—that is, Mr. Clock's—house. They all call him Mr. Clock now. I heard them talking and learned that all the time Mr. Jeeters has been living in the house he's been hunting for a secret hiding place of some kind. Please promise to tell them everything you know, Bob, so they'll let us go and Mom will be all right."

"The trouble is, I don't know anything," Bob told him. "That is, we solved one message. But all it said was to see some book, and we haven't any idea what book. That's as far as we got."

"They'll be awfully angry," Harry said "They were sure you'd have solved the messages by now. They've been checking up, and they think you three guys are pretty smart."

"Jupe's the one who's smart," Bob sighed. "Maybe if I convince them I don't know anything they'll let us go. After all, it won't do them any good to hold us if we don't know anything, will it?"

On that hopeful note they fell silent. The van rolled along, making occasional turns, but they had no idea in which direction they were going. Finally, after what seemed a long time, it stopped. They heard a big door, like an overhead garage door, roll up. The van moved forward a few feet and stopped again. The door rolled down. Then the back of the van was unlocked and the little man, Jerry, spoke.

"Come on now, climb out, both of you," he said. "Act nice if you know what's good for you."

Bob went first, with Harry following. He stepped down on to a concrete floor and looked around him. They were inside a big double garage. The doors were tightly closed and the two windows, one on each side, had shades pulled down over them. A bare light bulb illuminated the place. The van was the only vehicle in the garage, but the other half of it was fitted up as a workshop, with a workbench, a blowlamp and other tools scattered about.

There were several chairs beside the work-bench, and Jerry pointed at them.

"Sit down," he said with an ugly grin. "Make yourselves comfortable."

They sat down. Mr. Jeeters, his long face pale and unpleasant in the overhead light, stepped out of the front of the van, followed by the dapper, smiling Carlos.

"A rope round them to hold them securely," Mr. Jeeters ordered Jerry. "Then we'll talk."

Deftly Jerry looped some rope from the work-bench round their chests and tied them to the backs of the chairs. Mr. Jeeters drew up another chair, lit a big cigar, and puffed smoke at them.

"I assume Harry has told you what we want?" he asked Bob.

"He said you wanted to know the meaning of the messages," Bob said, his voice slightly shaky.

"That's just what we want. Those messages are the clue to the hiding place of something rather valuable," Mr. Jeeters growled. "We know all about how you got them—how you traced the screaming clock to Bert Clock and then to Rex King and tracked down the others with the messages Bert Clock sent them. Now we want to know what the messages say."

"Personally," Carlos put in, "I'd like to know the meaning of this nonsense of sending a

109

screaming clock to Rex King, and messages to the others. What was Bert up to?"

"He's the only one that knows that," Jerry spoke up. "Bert has a very twisty kind of mind, believe me. He was always great at making a plan, then letting other people carry it out and take the risks. We'll never know exactly what he was up to until we find him, and he seems to have disappeared without any trace."

"Jerry's right," Mr. Jeeters growled. "No use wondering what Bert was up to. Let's concentrate on finding the loot. Now boy, no more fooling around. What did those messages say?"

Bob swallowed hard.

"Well, the first message," he said, "was, '*I suggest you see the book.*' That's all. Just the one line."

"I suggest you see the book." Mr. Jeeters gnawed his lip. "All right, what book?"

"I don't know. The message didn't say."

"The second message probably did." Mr. Jeeters was getting impatient. "What did the second message say?"

"I don't know," Bob gulped. "We didn't work on it. Everybody was tired so we decided to wait until to-morrow."

"Careful, boy!" Mr. Jeeters said, and his tone was menacing. "Don't lie to me! I want to know what that second message said!"

"I tell you I don't know!" Bob answered.

"We didn't work on it. We were going to tackle it first thing to-morrow."

"Maybe he's telling the truth," Carlos suggested.

"Maybe," Mr. Jeeters agreed darkly. "It's possible. All right, boy, let's get on to the third message. The one that's all numbers. I have part of it, the part that Carlos got from your fat friend."

He took a torn sheet of paper from his pocket and held it in front of Bob's face.

"What do these numbers mean?"

"I don't know," Bob had to say. "Jupiter didn't have any idea."

Mr. Jeeters was looking very ugly. However, he seemed to realize Bob was telling the truth, and so did the others.

"We should have waited," Carlos said. "But if we had, and these interfering boys had led the police to the hiding place, we could have done nothing about it. The question is, what do we do next?"

"Obviously," Mr. Jeeters growled, "we need the other messages. If these boys can solve them, so can we. All we have to do is get our hands on the messages and we're set. Who has them, boy?"

"Jupiter Jones has them put away," Bob said. "And Jupiter is in bed by now."

"Well, he'll just have to get out of bed," Mr. Jeeters said grimly. "An idea is coming to me.

111

We'll just have your fat friend bring the messages to us and we'll all solve them together."

"How do you propose to get him here?" Carlos asked, looking thoughtful.

"He's fond of his friend, isn't he?" Mr. Jeeters asked, gesturing at Bob. "He wouldn't want anything to happen to him. I'm sure he'll be glad to bring us the messages. Don't you think so, boy?" he asked.

"I don't know," Bob said miserably. He had been hoping that when Mr. Jeeters and the others learned he didn't know anything more about the messages, he and Harry would be released. Now they were planning to get their hands on Jupiter instead!

"I think he will," Mr. Jeeters said. "We'll get the same result, only it will take us a little longer. First we have to make sure your parents aren't worrying about you. You'll telephone them to say you are spending the night with your friend Jupiter. Then you'll phone your fat companion and tell him that if he wants to see you again, he'll have to follow orders without telling anyone.

"Jerry, hand him the telephone!"

The little man picked up the phone that sat on the workbench and thrust it at Bob.

"Take it, kid!"

"I won't!" refused Bob stubbornly. "I won't telephone anybody. I've told everything I know and—and——" He swallowed hard, then finished, "And that's that!"

"Jerry." Mr. Jeeters glance went to the workbench. "I see a blowlamp over there. Light it and hand it to me."

The small man did as requested. In a moment Mr. Jeeters held the blowlamp in his hand, a bright yellow flame hissing from it. He brought it towards Bob, until Bob could feel the heat on his face and had to close his eyes against the brilliant light.

"Now, my boy," Mr. Jeeters said very softly, "would you rather telephone or would you rather have a blowlamp haircut? You have five seconds to make up your mind."

16

An Unexpected Meeting

"JUPE, I'M IN A BAD JAM!" Bob's urgent voice came over the telephone in Headquarters. "I need help."

"What's happened, Bob?" Jupiter asked tensely.

"Carlos and Jerry and Mr. Jeeters have me," said Bob, "and they've got Harry, too."

He went on to recount exactly what had happened. He finished by saying, "They made me call Mom and Dad and tell them I am staying with you to-night. Mr. Jeeters says you can ask your aunt and uncle for permission to come and visit me, and get away without anyone suspecting anything. He says that if you don't bring the messages to him, without telling anybody, we'll —well, we'll pay for it.

"But he swears that if you bring the messages, he'll let us all go as soon as they get what they want. Jupe, what do you think? Do you think you ought to do what they ask? Maybe you ought to call the police and——"

Over the phone there was the sound of a slap. Jupiter heard Bob gasp. Then Mr. Jeeter's voice came on the line.

"You heard your pal," he said. "If you want to see him again with nothing missing, like a couple of fingers or an ear, you do what I say. You get those messages and be waiting out front of that junkyard in exactly half an hour. I'm sending a van to pick you up. Don't tell anybody, you get me? That way you'll be all right in the end."

"All right, Mr. Jeeters," Jupiter said. "I shall obey orders to the letter. I will be waiting for your van in half an hour."

"You'd better," the man growled. Jupiter hung up very thoughtfully. He was tempted to call Pete, but there was no use involving Pete if it wasn't necessary. Jupiter decided that probably Mr. Jeeters meant what he had said. If he got the messages and found whatever mysterious object he was looking for, he wouldn't have any reason not to let them go.

Jupiter put the messages—the two he had solved and the torn one he couldn't make anything of—in the pocket of his shirt. Then, just before he let himself down into Tunnel Two, he scrawled on a piece of paper, *"Look for us in the room of clocks,"* and put that on top of the desk. The message was—well, it was just in case. He was pretty sure the room of clocks was the centre of this mystery.

That done, he crawled out through Tunnel Two and started towards Green Gate One. He had just reached it when a dark shadow seemed to detach itself from a pile of junk and move towards him. Jupiter had very quick reactions and he flung himself against Green Gate One, trying to pop through it and get away. But he wasn't fast enough. A powerful arm went around his chest. A hand closed over his mouth, almost suffocating him. And a voice whispered mockingly in his ear:

"So! We meet again. And this time I think I have the advantage."

The voice had a slight French accent. Jupiter recognized it instantly. It was Hugenay, the in-

A hand closed over Jupiter's mouth . . .

ternational art thief! The Three Investigators had encountered Hugenay, the debonair, clever European, once before, in an earlier case,* and Jupiter would never forget him. He still remembered with a little chill the fog-shrouded old graveyard where Hugenay had made him and Pete prisoners.

"I deduce," Hugenay whispered into his ear, "that you remember me. You know then that I am not a man to be trifled with. If I release you, will you remain quiet for a moment's conversation? I dislike making threats, but if you do attempt an outcry, I will have to—silence you."

Jupiter managed to nod his head. Seeming satisfied, Hugenay took his hand from Jupiter's mouth. By the faint light, Jupiter could just see the man's face. Hugenay was smiling slightly.

"You seem surprised to see me again," he said softly. "You should have realized that when half a million dollars in stolen paintings was at stake, Hugenay would not be far off."

"Stolen paintings?" Jupiter exclaimed. "Is that what we're all looking for?"

"You didn't know?" Now Hugenay seemed surprised. "Five wonderful canvases, with a total value of half a million dollars, stolen more than two years ago and lost ever since—that's what I'm after. Surely you must have known, or why go to so much effort?"

* The Mystery of the Stuttering Parrot.

117

"We were investigating a screaming clock," Jupiter said. "It led us to some clues and I guessed there was something valuable hidden, but I didn't know what it was."

"Oh yes, that clock," Hugenay answered. "I have been wondering about that clock. I have taken it completely apart——"

"You're the one who stole it?" Jupiter asked. "It was you who chased Bob and Harry yesterday?"

"Indeed it was," Hugenay told him. "I also had men following you, but the fools lost you. I got the clock when that officer so obligingly took your friends to the police station and they left it in the parked car outside. But I have taken it completely apart, looking for a clue of some sort hidden in it, possibly engraved upon the works, without finding anything. Now I must know what is in those messages your ingenious organization has recovered."

"Why should I tell you?" Jupe asked, his boldness returning. "If I yell now, Hans and Konrad will be here in a minute, and they'll tear you apart."

Hugenay chuckled. "I like spirit in a boy," he said. "However, it should stop short of utter rashness. I am not alone and—But why make threats? I have something to offer you for your co-operation. Help me, and I'll help you."

"Help me how?"

"The boy Harry whom you met at Bert Clock's house. His father is in prison. I will enable you to prove he is innocent. I will take the paintings—you will get an innocent man out of jail. Surely you won't refuse to do that?"

Jupiter thought furiously. Then he nodded. "All right, I'll help if you'll do that. But there's one thing more you'll have to do."

"And what is that, my plump but clever young friend?"

Jupiter told him exactly what had happened to Bob and what the situation was—that he was supposed to be picked up by a van in less than half an hour to take him to the place where Mr. Jeeters and the others had Bob and Harry.

Hugenay uttered a few expressive words in French.

"Those idiots!" he said. "I did not think they would act so swiftly. I planned to get the pictures and be gone before they could do anything!"

"You knew about them?" Jupiter asked, puzzled.

"Certainly I knew about them. I know far more than you think. I have been in the city for two weeks, casting about for a clue. I have—certain methods. If you wish, you may assume that I have had the telephone wires of these individuals tapped and listened to all their secret conversations—however, I will not say yes or no to that. Obviously, though, there has been a change in plans to-day. We must foil those plans.

"Yes, boy, I will help you rescue your friends, then we will find those paintings, and by this time tomorrow I will be five thousand miles away. You must start by following instructions. At the proper time you must be waiting outside for the van. Get in and go with the driver. I and my men will follow behind, discreetly. Leave the rest to me. The less you know, the better "

Realizing that he had to trust Hugenay, Jupiter eased out through Green Gate One and went back to his home. He was beginning to be a little sorry he'd ever thought of investigating a screaming clock, but it was too late to change things. Anyway, he knew that Hugenay was very clever and resourceful, and he felt sure that the Frenchman could outwit Mr. Jeeters and Jerry and Carlos.

Jupiter entered the house, where his aunt and uncle were watching television. He told them Bob had phoned and wanted to see him. They readily gave him permission to spend the night with Bob, and Jupe went up to his room. He put on a warm jacket and thrust the messages into the inside pocket.

Downstairs, he said good night to his aunt and uncle and then walked out to stand in front of the main gates of the salvage yard.

Hugenay was waiting there for him. He came

over and put his hand on Jupiter's shoulder and spoke earnestly.

"Don't forget we're working together now," he said. "First we have to get Bob and Harry free. When the van comes, get in and don't give any sign you know I am following you. If in any way they get suspicious. I leave it to your cleverness to know what to say. Now I am leaving you."

He faded away into the darkness. If he had a car waiting, Jupiter could not see it. Possibly it was hidden at the other end of the salvage yard. Jupiter waited. It was very quiet and dark here beyond the outskirts of town, and he shivered a little.

Headlights cut the darkness. A small van came slowly down the street. For a moment the headlights shone clearly on him. The van stopped. The door opened and the little man, Jerry, leaned out.

"All right, kid, hop in!" he rasped. "And for your own sake, and your pals', you'd better not be trying any tricks!"

17

In the Hands of the Enemy

THE VAN MOVED steadily along in the direction of Hollywood. Carlos was driving, and Jupiter was squeezed in between him and Jerry.

"You have those messages with you, boy?" Carlos demanded.

"Yes, sir, I have them," Jupiter said, sounding unusually meek and humble.

"That's good," Jerry muttered. "Because if— what is it, Carlos?"

Carlos was staring into the rear-view mirror.

"I think we're being followed. There's been a car behind us for the last couple of miles!"

"Followed!" Jerry exclaimed. He grabbed Jupiter, hard. "Kid, if you called the cops——"

"No, sir, I didn't!" Jupiter sounded frightened, and only part of it was acting. They had spotted Hugenay's car, and the whole plan with Hugenay was in danger of failing.

"Then if it isn't the police, who is it?" Carlos demanded. "Quick, answer me! Don't stall or I'll know you're lying!"

"If we're being followed," Jupiter said rapidly,

"it might be somebody else who wants the messages, too. Somebody stole the screaming clock yesterday. If it wasn't you, that shows somebody else is interested, and that same person might have been watching my house and seen you pick me up. Naturally he'd want to know where I was going."

"That's it!" Jerry exclaimed. "That clock—Harry told Jeeters all about it. I'll bet the kid's right. Someone else is trying to find the loot. Carlos, you've got to shake them."

"Leave it to me," Carlos said grimly. "There's a freeway only a mile ahead and I'll get on to it. Then let them try to follow!"

He maintained the same speed for another couple of minutes. Then, as they approached the freeway, he put on speed, dashed up an entry ramp, and a moment later was in the midst of a stream of fast-moving traffic heading towards Hollywood.

The freeways of Los Angeles and Hollywood are a great network of concrete highways which connect the city of Los Angeles and the surrounding territory. A tremendous number of cars stream along them all day and most of the night. Now they were on a six-lane highway, and all six lanes contained cars and trucks moving at great speed.

Carlos stepped on the accelerator and began to cut in and out of the traffic. In a minute or two anyone following would be hopelessly lost among the cars and huge trucks. Carlos, however, was not satisfied until he had been threading in and out of the dense traffic for ten minutes. Then he cut to the outer lane and swung sharply down an exit ramp.

He slowed as he hit the city street below them and watched the rear-view mirror intently. Apparently he was satisfied, for after a few moments he relaxed.

"Nobody followed us out of that exit," he said. "If anyone was tailing us, we've lost them."

As Carlos proceeded at a normal speed, Jupiter's spirits sank steadily lower. He had been counting on Hugenay. Now Hugenay had lost them, and could be of no help.

The van turned into a driveway between two old houses. In the rear was a large, two-car garage. Carlos peeped the horn once, and one of the sliding doors went up. The van eased inside and the door went down again.

Carlos and Jerry climbed out, hustling Jupiter along. Jupiter saw Mr. Jeeters waiting for them, and behind him Bob and Harry, tied to chairs.

"Any trouble?" Mr. Jeeters asked. "You're a little late."

"Someone followed us," Carlos reported. "We had to take time to throw them off the trail. The kid swears it wasn't cops. May have been whoever stole the screaming clock yesterday Anyway, whoever it was, we lost them."

"Good." Mr. Jeeters fixed hard eyes on Jupiter. "I'm sure our young friend here is too smart to have been trying any tricks. All right, boy, now the messages. Let's have them."

Jupiter fumbled in his pocket. He brought out a piece of paper.

"Here's the first message, Mr. Jeeters."

Jeeters took it and read it. *"I suggest you see the book.* Yes, your friend already told us that one. What book does it mean?"

"I don't know."

"Well, doesn't the second message tell us?"

"Here it is, sir. You can see what it says."

"Humph! *Only a room where Father Time hums.* What does that mean?"

"I deduce that it means Mr. Clock's library, where all those electrified clocks hum as they work."

"Yes, yes, of course, it has to mean that. But I've been all over that room, looking for sliding panels, concealed hiding places, anything, and I found nothing. Well, give me the rest of the third message. I already have half." And he displayed a torn piece of paper.

Jupiter was fumbling in his pocket when there was an unexpected interruption. With a great breaking of glass, the windows on each side of the garage crashed in. The shades flew up.

Seconds later a blue-uniformed man was climbing in through each window, each holding a large automatic pointed at Mr. Jeeters, Carlos and Jerry.

"Up with your hands!" the first policeman snapped. "Quick! No false moves!"

"The cops!" Jerry exclaimed. Carlos muttered something in Spanish whose meaning the boys did not know but could guess.

"Stand still! Put your hands up!" the second policeman ordered. "We have you covered from both sides."

Slowly Jerry and Carlos put up their hands. Mr. Jeeters backed up until he was against the workbench and for a moment it seemed as if he was feeling for a weapon behind him. But the first policeman covered him with his gun.

"You, too!" he snapped. "You—what're you doing? What's that burning?"

"He's burned the messages!" Jupiter exclaimed. The blowlamp was still burning on the bench with a low flame, and Mr. Jeeters had thrust all the messages into its flame. Even as they watched the bits of paper turned into curls of ash.

"Now, let's see you try to solve anything!" Mr. Jeeters sneered.

"I can remember the first two messages," Jupiter said. "But if the one with all the numbers is gone, I don't know how we can ever find out what Mr. Clock was trying to tell us."

"Try your brains on that problem!" Mr. Jeeters laughed. He turned to Jerry and Carlos. "You fools!" he hissed at the other two. "You told me you had shaken off your tail This fat kid called the police, and you let them trail you here——"

"But I didn't!" Jupiter blurted out, as astonished as anyone else by this new development.

"Keep them covered, Joe," the first policeman said.

He strode to the garage door and swung it up. A dapper-looking man stepped in, and the garage door swung down behind him. He stood smiling at the group before him.

"Well, well," he said. "Nicely done, men. The situation seems to be under control."

Jupiter's eyes bugged out.

"Mr. Hugenay!" he gasped.

18

Back to the Room of Clocks

"YES, MY BOY," Hugenay said. "It is I, the incomparable Hugenay, who has foiled the police of three continents. You did not think I would let dullards like these get ahead of me, did you?"

Mr. Jeeters and his companions seemed to recognize the name, for they looked grim and nervous. They remained silent, however, waiting for developments.

"But—but——" Jupiter spluttered. "They lost you in the traffic. You couldn't possibly have followed us!"

"I took precautions," Hugenay said airily. He stepped up to Jupiter and slid a hand into the side pocket of Jupe's jacket. He brought out a small, flat object.

"This," he said, "is an electronic signalling device. I put it in your pocket the last time I spoke to you. In my car I have a receiver tuned to it. I simply followed the sound it emitted. Even in the traffic on the freeway I was able to follow, and I knew when the truck turned off. It took me a few minutes to trail the sound to this garage, but once I had located you, I simply sent my assistants in to take charge."

"Mr. Hugenay!" It was Bob who spoke now. Still tied to a chair, he had been staring at the art thief ever since he had entered. "It was you who chased us yesterday and stole the clock, wasn't it?"

Mr. Hugenay made a slight bow.

"I plead guilty. However, I intended no harm. I only wanted to, shall we say, help you in your search? But this is no time for talking, pleasant though it is to meet old acquaintances again. Men, handcuff those three to that post."

A steel post rose in the centre of the garage to support the roof. Cowed by the policemen's guns, Mr. Jeeters, Jerry and Carlos stood with their backs to it while one of the blue-coated men manacled their wrists. The right wrist of each man was handcuffed to the left wrist of the man beside him, so that when the policemen had finished, the three made a circle around the steel post, quite unable to go anywhere.

"Very good," Hugenay said. "Now it is time for us to get on with our business."

"Wait a minute, Hugenay." It was Jeeters who spoke, and he was trying to sound pleasant. "Why don't we all throw in together? Between us we can probably find the stuff a lot quicker."

"I know everything you know," Hugenay said lightly. "You tried to get ahead of me and you must suffer for it. In any case, as you see I am working with the police now. All right, men, untie the boys and let's get started for Bert Clock's library."

A moment later the six were in a large black sedan, moving at a normal speed through the Hollywood streets.

Hugenay chuckled to himself as they rode along.

"My boy," he said to Jupiter, who sat beside

him, "no doubt you had given up all thought of ever seeing me again."

"Well, yes sir, I had," Jupiter admitted. "Especially after the police came through the windows. I never expected you to be working with the police."

Hugenay chuckled again. "The police? I merely rented two police uniforms at a costume shop to-day and presto!—I had two policemen for assistants. Do not be fooled by surface appearances."

Jupiter gulped. He *had* been fooled—just as much fooled as Carlos and the others. His reluctant admiration for Hugenay rose.

"Harry," Jupiter said to the boy who was squeezed in beside him, "we are co-operating with Mr. Hugenay. I agreed to do so if he would help get you and Bob free. He has done that. Also he has said he will do one thing more—he'll prove your father is innocent."

"He will?" Harry exclaimed. "Golly, that's terrific!"

"It is simple, my boy," Hugenay said. "I will tell you the circumstances. Mr. Bert Clock, the former actor, has—if you have not already guessed it—been the brains behind a gang of art thieves that has been operating for years in this area, stealing valuable paintings from wealthy motion picture people who did not guard them well enough."

"Of course!" Bob said. "That's why Mr. Clock changed his name some years ago and has been acting so mysterious. He's a thief. I'll bet he stole those paintings that were hidden under the linoleum in Harry's kitchen."

"Perhaps he did not steal them himself," Hugenay said as they rolled along. "He had assistants to do that. Jerry, the former jockey, was one. He used several jockeys, because they are small men and can get through windows easily. He sold the pictures to wealthy South American collectors who would keep them safely hidden. Carlos was a contact with the South Americans.

"A couple of years ago, several paintings were stolen that Mr. Clock could not get rid of. Two of his best South American customers had just been put in jail after the failure of a plot to overthrow their government. So Mr. Clock hid the paintings, and told his men he would sell them later, when the time was ripe.

"However, he made no move and Jerry and Carlos decided to act on their own. They stole three paintings and brought them to Mr. Clock to sell, demanding that he also produce the five —yes, it was five—that were hidden.

"However, by one of those freakish coincidences with which life is full, the police investigating this latest art robbery turned their attention to someone in Mr. Clock's own house—your father, Harry. Frightened lest they learn too much, Mr. Clock hid the three new paintings where the police would find them and blame your father."

"He framed my father!" Harry said bitterly. "And Mom and I always thought he was such a nice guy."

"Yes, he framed your father. Then, shortly after that, he vanished. I believe Carlos and Jerry and perhaps Jeeters were pressing him too hard. He didn't dare bring the missing pictures out of hiding, so he left for South America and hid himself. From everyone but me, that is. I have connections all over the world, if I may boast a bit.

"I contacted him, suggesting he let me have the pictures to handle—you see, I had made it my business to learn all about his activities—but he refused. He was sick, in fact he was dying, and he was feeling remorse about your father, Harry. He sent off the strange screaming clock and several messages to various old friends, and then he died."

"But *why* did he send the messages and the clock, Mr. Hugenay?" Bob asked. "Wouldn't it have been simpler just to write a letter to the police?"

"Bert Clock was never a simple man," Mr. Hugenay said. "He did it the way he did for some reason. Perhaps we will guess that reason when we decode the strange messages."

"But Mr. Jeeters burned the messages," Jupiter reminded him. "He burned all of the first two and half of the third message."

"But naturally you remember them?" Hugenay asked, a trifle anxious.

"I remember the first two," Jupiter admitted. "But the third was all numbers. I couldn't possibly remember it. Anyway, I only saw it once, then Carlos got the bottom half from me. The first message said, *'I suggest you see the book'* and the second message said, *'Only a room where Father Time hums'*."

"Book?" Hugenay frowned. "What book, I wonder? The room where time hums is simple enough, of course. It can only be the room of many clocks. I assumed all along our starting point would be there. Well, here we are Once we are inside we can ponder the message further."

The car stopped at the kerb. They all got out and walked up the path to the home of Bert Clock. Harry let them in and went to look for his mother.

As he called her name, they heard a pounding on the cellar door. He quickly unlocked it and Mrs. Smith emerged.

"Thank goodness you came, Harry!" she said. "That awful Mr. Jeeters and his friends! They locked me in the cellar and said I'd have to stay there until they got back. I see you have some policemen with you. Well, I want them arrested right away!"

"They have been taken care of, madam," Mr. Hugenay said, making a bow. "Indeed, we are here on business that vitally concerns you."

"This is Mr. Hugenay!" Harry said excitedly. "He says he can prove Dad is innocent."

"Really? That's wonderful!" his mother exclaimed.

"In order to do that," Mr. Hugenay said, "we must be allowed into Mr. Clock's—or Mr. Hadley's if you prefer the name he used—library. We may have to do some damage. I assure you it is necessary to prove your husband innocent. Have we your permission?"

"Yes, of course. Anything!" Mrs. Smith said happily. "Tear the house down if it will clear Ralph."

"Thank you. Now I shall ask you and Harry and Bob to remain outside the library while I and my men are at work. You will communicate with no one. If the telephone rings, do not answer it. Is it agreed?"

"Yes indeed. The boys and I will stay in the kitchen and have a bite to eat—I haven't eaten for hours. Go right ahead, Mr. Hugenay."

"Thank you," Hugenay said and turned to Jupiter. "Lead us to the library, my boy."

Meanwhile, unaware of the excitement into which Bob and Jupiter had been plunged, Pete was at home watching television with his father. Mr. Crenshaw was a technical expert with the motion picture industry, and often travelled to the far corners of the world to help make films.

Pete was having trouble keeping his mind on the TV detective story. He was still thinking about the mystery of Mr. Clock and his strange clock. As the programme ended, he asked his father a question.

"Did I know Bert Clock?" his father replied. "I certainly did. Not well, of course, but I ran into him on a couple of pictures. What a screamer that fellow was! Made your blood turn cold. There was an old picture—oh, back twenty years ago, I guess, in which he pulled a very interesting trick."

"Trick!" Pete idly reached for a potato chip from the bowl on the table and munched on it. He loved potato chips. "What kind of trick, Dad?"

"What?" his father asked, already watching the next programme. Pete repeated the question. His father, absorbed in an exciting Western, answered somewhat absent-mindedly. Pete blinked. This was something Jupiter didn't know. Pete couldn't see how it possibly fitted in, but Jupe liked to know everything possible about his cases. Maybe he ought to call Jupe and tell him.

Even if First was in bed, he'd want to know.

"It's getting late," Mr. Crenshaw said abruptly. "Time for you to be in bed, boy. Up you go!"

"Okay, Dad," Pete agreed and went off to bed without phoning. He could tell Jupe when he saw him in the morning.

19

A Fruitless Search

INSIDE THE ROOM of clocks, Mr. Hugenay became very business-like. He directed his two men to pull the shades tightly. Then he switched on all the lights and surveyed the room.

"Hundreds of books," he murmured. "Three paintings, probably worthless. A large mirror. Many clocks. Some panelled walls where a hiding place could be concealed. Now the first message tells us to see a book. The second message directs us to this room where time hums. The third message—let me see the third message, boy."

Jupiter handed him the torn top half of the third message. Hugenay looked at the numbers and scowled.

"Reference to words on certain pages of a

book, obviously," he said. "But meaningless without the proper book. Boy, what book do you think it might be?"

"I haven't any idea, sir," Jupiter replied. "Though it's probably a book in this room somewhere."

"Yes, I think so, too. Let us look at a few."

Hugenay went to the nearest shelf, pulled out three or four books and glanced through them. He thrust them back.

"Pah!" he said. "They mean nothing There are too many books to look at every one. Yet we must have the message. Think, boy, think. You're supposed to be good at thinking."

Jupiter pinched his lip to make his thoughts come faster.

"Mr. Hugenay——" he said at last.

"Yes, boy?"

"These messages were meant for Rex King He was supposed to solve them. Therefore it seems logical that he would know what book Mr. Clock meant."

"Of course he'll know! We only have to telephone him and ask him."

"But he's in the hospital."

"That is bad." Hugenay's face fell. "Try another idea."

"We could ask his wife. She might know."

"Of course. Sound thinking. Phone her and ask her."

"I'd better have Bob ask her," Jupiter said. "He talked to her."

He led the way to the kitchen, where Bob was having cocoa with Mrs. Smith and Harry.

"Find anything, First?" he asked.

"Not yet. We need your assistance." Jupe explained what he wanted Bob to do. Bob went to the telephone in the hall, looked up Rex King's number, and dialled. He recognized Mrs. King's voice when she answered.

He told her about the mysterious book Bert Clock had referred to in the message. It was probably a book that her husband would have known about. Could she suggest any book which Bert Clock would have referred to as *the* book?

"Yes, I think so," Mrs. King said. "A good many years ago, Bert wrote a book about his experiences in radio. My husband helped him some with the writing. It was called *A Clock Screams at Midnight*. Does that help?"

"It certainly does!" Bob exclaimed. "Thank you very much." He hung up and relayed the news to Jupiter and Mr. Hugenay. They whirled back into the library and closed the door. Bob went back to the kitchen to wait some more, wondering what this new development would uncover.

After a couple of minutes of scanning the shelves, Hugenay snatched up a book.

"Here it is," he said. *"A Clock Screams at Midnight,* by Albert Clock. Now we are making progress. Where is that message? Let me see— page number 3, word number 27. I will look for it. You, boy, write the words down as I proceed."

He leafed through the book to page 3 and counted words.

"The word is *'stand,'* " he reported. "Now for the rest."

He worked rapidly. Jupiter wrote down each word as they found it.

Presently Hugenay came to the end of the torn message. "That's all," he said. "The rest of the message is gone. Read what we have."

Jupiter read the message aloud. *"Stand in the middle of the room at one minute to midnight. Have two detectives and two reporters with you. Hold hands, making a circle, and keep absolutely silent for one minute. At midnight exactly——"* He stopped. "That's where the message ends, Mr. Hugenay."

"A thousand thunders! It ends just before it tells us anything. At midnight exactly—*what?* What is supposed to happen? There's no way to tell. That Bert Clock had a very clever mind. We can't guess what he was thinking."

He sighed. "There's nothing for it," he said. "We'll just have to tear the room apart. Either the pictures are hidden in this room, or perhaps there's a key to a storage vault hidden here. It would help if we knew what we were looking for but, as we don't, we'll make the best of it."

"Wait, Mr. Hugenay!" Jupiter said. "Could the pictures be those pictures on the wall? I mean, could the real pictures have had new pictures painted over them?"

"No, no, I'm sure that's not the case, but I'll look."

Hugenay took down the nearest picture and examined it closely. He scraped the paint at one corner with his penknife.

"No, just a worthless picture," he said. "We'll start by leafing through all the other books, to see if there is a concealed key. Then we'll examine the walls and the bookcases for hidden cupboards or sliding panels."

"Wait!" Jupiter pleaded. "I've had another idea, sir."

"Another? Your mind hums like a top!" Hugenay exclaimed. "What is it this time?"

"I think I know of a way we might get the rest of the message in the book, sir."

"Well, then let's have it!"

"When people pick out words in a book to make a message," Jupiter said, "they often put a pencil mark beneath the word to help them count down to it. If the message words in Mr. Clock's book have pencil marks under them, we can find the rest of the message by looking through the book till we see more words marked with pencil."

"Remarkable cogitation," Hugenay said. "Let us check and see."

Quickly he looked through Mr. Clock's book again.

"You're right, boy! Each word of the message has a small pencil dot beneath it. Here—you look for the rest of the message."

Jupiter took the book and turned each page slowly, looking only for a tiny pencil dot. Presently he came to a word. He called it out and Hugenay wrote it down. It took quite a while to go through the book page by page, but Jupiter was interested in the job and did not pause.

At last Jupiter could find no more marks.

"Very well," Hugenay said. "I'll read the whole message. '*Stand in the middle of the room at one minute to midnight. Have two detectives and two reporters with you. Hold hands, making a circle, and keep absolutely silent for one minute. At midnight exactly the alarm of the screaming clock which I sent you should go off. Have it set at full volume. Let the scream continue until my hiding place is uncovered*'."

Mr. Hugenay looked at Jupiter.

"What do you suppose it means?" he asked.

Jupiter frowned. It was one of the strangest messages he had ever encountered.

"It sounds to me," he said, "as if the screaming clock will make some kind of mechanism work that will open a hidden panel, or something like that. Locks can be made that will open only at special sounds. Some will open only if the owner speaks to them. I think Mr. Clock's scream must do something like that."

"Exactly," Hugenay agreed. "My own conclusion. A trick lock opened by a special sound."

"Now," Jupiter said, "if you have the clock, we can try it out. I don't think that business about holding hands or waiting for midnight means anything. It's just atmosphere."

"There is, unfortunately, a difficulty," Hugenay said slowly. "The clock no longer exists. I took it apart looking for a hidden message engraved inside it. It won't scream any more." He sighed. "I did not anticipate this. It is one of the few times I have been guilty of a grave error. But it can't be helped. The clock is gone."

"Then," Jupiter said, "I don't know what we can do."

"There is a way," Hugenay said. "It is crude and I detest crudeness, but this time it is necessary. My men will open up all the walls in this room, including those behind the bookcases. If there is a secret cupboard or other hiding place we will find it.

"Fred," he said to one of his men. "Go out to the car and bring in the tools. We have work to do."

20

Startling Developments

MR. CLOCK'S LIBRARY was a mess. It looked as if a bomb had exploded or a demolition squad had started to demolish the house. The latter was almost correct. Certainly Hugenay's men had wrecked the room. They had attacked it with chisels, drills, axes and crowbars.

First they had removed all the books from the shelves, stacking them on the floor, and taken down the pictures and mirror. Then they had opened up the walls, methodically. They had examined every section of the room for an opening behind the wall. They had ripped down some of the bookshelves looking for a secret door, or a hidden closet. They had even attacked the ceiling until they found it was solid plaster.

All of their efforts had ended in failure. They hadn't found anything remotely resembling a secret hiding place.

Hugenay looked angry as well as disappointed.

"Well," he said. "We have failed. Bert Clock has hidden something so well I cannot find it. I would not have believed it possible."

They had found nothing resembling a secret hiding place.

144

"Does that mean you can't prove Harry's father is innocent?" Jupiter asked.

"Not without finding the stolen pictures, boy," Hugenay replied. "And as you can see, we have not found them. Unless you have some more ideas."

Now Jupiter was pinching his lip. An idea *was* coming to him.

"Mr. Hugenay," he said. "The clock is destroyed, but maybe the scream isn't."

"What do you mean by that?"

"There's a man, a Mr. Gerald Watson, who has a collection of tapes of all the radio shows Mr. Clock did in the series, *A Scream at Midnight*. Each of them starts with a scream. Maybe this particular scream is recorded on one of the tapes. If it is and we can borrow the tape and tape recorder from Mr. Watson, we don't need the clock."

"Call him at once. Time is important!"

Jupiter went out and called Mr. Watson. Mr. Watson was puzzled at first, but he quickly recognized the scream Jupiter described.

"I know the very one you mean, yes indeed. My goodness, that scream made Bert famous, in an old film twenty years ago. Of course I have it on a tape. I can put my hands right on it. I'll be glad to lend you the tape and the recorder, but I insist, you must tell me later what this mystery is all about."

145

Jupiter promised and said a man would be right over and hung up. Bob and Harry and Mrs. Smith came out of the kitchen to listen, and were startled when they saw the mess in the library

"Golly, Jupe, you've really wrecked that room!" Bob said. "Did you find anything?"

"Not yet," Jupiter admitted.

"Why, it looks as if you're trying to tear the house down!" Mrs. Smith exclaimed. "I'd never have given you permission if I'd known you planned to do so much damage!"

"We are looking for evidence that will prove your husband innocent," Mr. Hugenay told her. "Do you wish us to stop without finding it?"

"Well, no, no, of course not," Mrs. Smith answered, flustered. "If you can prove he's innocent, I guess it's worth any amount of damage."

"We will try to do no more." Hugenay made a little bow, and she seemed satisfied.

They had already dug into all the walls looking for a hiding place, so now there was nothing to do but wait. The man named Joe had gone in the car for the tape recorder, and in about an hour he returned, lugging the heavy machine.

"Here it is," he said. "The old fellow put the tape on, so it's all ready to roll."

"Very well," Hugenay said. He turned to Jupiter, "Do you know how to run this apparatus?" he asked.

"Yes, sir." Jupiter opened the carrying case of the tape recorder, got out the electric connection, and plugged it in.

"Let's put the room back the way it was," he said. "I mean we can't really do it completely, but let's hang the pictures and the mirror and put some books back on the shelves."

Hugenay started to protest, but reconsidered.

"Do it, men," he said, and they obeyed instructions. They rehung the mirror and pictures, arranged some of the books in the bookcases, and stepped back, waiting.

"Now, some action, please!" Hugenay said impatiently. "I think we are wasting time, but let us at least try."

"Yes, sir." Jupiter had been running the tape at low volume, listening to it while the men worked. He had located the place on the tape where the scream came, and wound the tape back.

"Now I'm ready," he said. "Everyone please remain quiet."

He started the tape and turned up the volume. There were a few words of conversation between a man and woman. Then the scream came, high-pitched, desperate, and eerie. It rang through the room, and with a last despairing wail was silent.

All of them waited for a secret door to open or a panel to pop out of the wall.

Nothing whatever happened.

"I knew it!" Hugenay exclaimed. "I tell you, boy, there's no place in this room five valuable pictures could be hidden. No place!"

"I think there is, sir," Jupiter said, with sudden eagerness. He had noticed something the men hadn't and suddenly he thought he knew where the stolen pictures were hidden. It only remained to test his theory.

"Let's try it again," Jupiter said. "Perhaps the volume wasn't high enough."

He pushed the volume knob all the way round. Then he rewound the tape and started the scream once more.

This time it burst upon them as a screech of such terror that they put their hands over their ears. Up, up, up went the sound of the scream until it was almost unbearable.

Then it happened.

The glass in the large mirror on the wall cracked in a thousand pieces. Glass sprayed across the floor. In a second there was nothing left of the mirror but the frame and a few jagged pieces of glass sticking to it.

Where the mirror had been was a brilliantly coloured picture. As they watched, it curled forward and fell to the floor, followed by four more pictures that had been carefully sandwiched between the glass and the frame.

The purpose of the screaming clock was at last explained.

Heedless of the broken glass, Hugenay darted forward to snatch up the first picture, an abstract consisting of whirls of colour against a black background.

"The pictures!" he exclaimed in triumph. "Half a million dollars' worth, and at last I have them!"

At that moment, the library door opened, and a voice behind them said sharply, "Put up your hands! You're all under arrest!"

There was stunned silence as they all turned and stared at the group of men in the doorway. Two policemen stood with drawn revolvers. Behind them Jupiter recognized Police Chief Reynolds of Rocky Beach, and Mr. Crenshaw, Pete's father. Then Pete himself squirmed through the group into the room.

"Jupe!" he said anxiously. "Are you all right? Golly, we were worried about you! I couldn't get to sleep—I wanted to tell you something—so I telephoned your house. Your uncle said you were at Bob's, and Bob's mother thought you both were at your house, Jupiter. I called Headquarters, and you weren't there either. Then I rode over to Heaquarters to see if you had left any message. I found your note about the clock room, so I telephoned here, but nobody answered.

"Then I got worried. I told Dad you and Bob were missing and he called Chief Reynolds. We all came here to investigate and it looks like we came just in time."

Chief Reynolds stepped forward and took the picture which Hugenay was holding. He carefully placed it on the desk.

"This was stolen from a gallery about two years ago," he said. "I remember, photographs of it were circulated to police at the time."

He turned to Jupiter.

"I had a hunch this might be serious," he said. "I remembered about Bob being chased yesterday and something stolen from his car and figured you might be tangling with something big. Looks like we got here just in time to catch the thieves with the stolen goods."

Jupiter turned and looked at Mr. Hugenay. Considering that the art thief had just been captured after outwitting police for many years, he looked very calm. He was in fact smiling. Now he lowered his hands, took a cigar from his pocket and lit it.

"Tell me, please," he said, "with what crime am I charged?"

"Well, possession of stolen goods will be enough to start with," Chief Reynolds snapped. "Then maybe abduction, malicious damage—oh, we've got you on a lot of charges."

"Indeed?" Hugenay puffed on his cigar and

150

blew out a cloud of smoke. "Please do not make reckless accusations, my dear fellow. I came here in a public-spirited hunt for some stolen art treasures that had been hidden by Albert Clock. This boy——" he nodded at Jupiter, "will tell you that he and his friends were aiding me voluntarily with my search.

"The damage to this room was done by permission of the lady in charge of the house It was necessary to find the stolen paintings. We have found them. We will now turn them over to you, gentlemen, and take our leave."

"Now wait a minute——" Chief Reynolds began.

"Tell them I am speaking the exact truth, boy," Mr. Hugenay requested of Jupiter.

Jupe blinked. It was true, of course, everything Hugenay had said.

"Yes, Chief Reynolds," Jupiter said reluctantly. "We are here voluntarily and Mr. Hugenay was hunting for the hidden pictures. That's all absolutely true."

"But we know all about him. He was going to keep them when he found them!" Chief Reynolds cried.

"That is a matter of opinion," Hugenay said. "You cannot prove it. So if you will excuse us, we will take our leave now. You will not arrest us, I'm sure, because if you do I will file a suit for a million dollars for false arrest and I will win it."

He gestured to his men, who were still holding their hands up nervously.

"Come on, men," he said. "We are no longer needed here. We will say goodnight."

"Now wait a minute!" one of the policemen exclaimed. "You can't slip out as easily as all that. We can hold these men for impersonating police officers, anyway!"

"Really?" Mr. Hugenay yawned slightly. "Fred, please step forward. Now, gentlemen, examine the insignia Fred is wearing. Notice the initials."

"N-Y-P-D!" Chief Reynolds said, puzzled.

"Correct. Standing for New York Police Department. These men are actors, whom I hired to help me in this hunt. They are wearing uniforms of the police department of the City of New York, which is almost three thousand miles away. It is merely a harmless joke on my part. You can't say that they are impersonating Los Angeles police officers—not when they are wearing New York City police uniforms!"

Jupiter gulped. Now that he looked closely, it was true. Along with everyone else, he had taken it for granted the men were dressed as Los Angeles policemen.

"Come, gentlemen," Hugenay said and started

calmly towards the door. Chief Reynolds scratched his head.

"Darned if I can think of anything to arrest them for!" he said, in frustration. "I guess we'll have to let them go."

Jupiter shook his head admiringly. Hugenay hadn't got the pictures he had been after, but he was certainly making a clean getaway once again.

At the doorway, Hugenay paused. He looked back at Jupiter.

"It was a pleasure working with you, my boy," he said. "I am only sorry we can't work together professionally. With my training you would have a great future. Still, I am sure we will meet again some day."

In a moment the outer door opened and closed and Hugenay and his men were gone. Chief Reynolds was still scratching his head.

"Well," he said, "I think it's time for some explanations. Jupiter, just what is this whole thing all about?"

Jupiter drew a deep breath.

"Well, Chief Reynolds, it all started with a screaming clock. You see——"

And he talked for quite a long time.

Alfred Hitchcock Speaking

IT IS NOT necessary to relate all that Jupiter Jones told Chief Reynolds and the others However, you might be interested in a few details that emerged before the case was officially closed.

The stolen pictures which had caused Harry's father's arrest had been put under the linoleum by Mr. Clock himself, who was afraid the police might suspect him unless they had someone else to pin the guilt on. As soon as he safely could, Mr. Clock had then left the country and gone into hiding in South America. He wanted both to get away from further police attention and to escape from Carlos, Jerry and Mr. Jeeters, members of the gang that had stolen the pictures who were pressing him to resume activity again.

Mr. Clock had died of an illness in South America, as Hugenay had reported, so it was impossible to bring him to justice. As for Carlos, Jerry and Mr. Jeeters, they were taken into custody in the garage where they had been left handcuffed. They admitted their part in the burglary ring, and cleared Harry's father of any guilt whatever. He was released from prison, and reunited with his family.

The trick that Bert Clock did in the old film, and which both Pete's father and Mr. Watson remembered, was to shatter a mirror by screaming in front of it in high-pitched tones. The vibrations caused by certain sound waves can shatter thin glass, and this made a very dramatic scene in the film.

Mr. Clock had obtained a similar mirror later and hung it in his library. He used it as the hiding place for stolen pictures until they were sold. The five he could not sell he left there, as it was the safest hiding place he knew. His reasons for wanting the mirror can only be guessed. It is my belief that he enjoyed knowing he could shatter the glass with a scream any time he wanted to, and perhaps intended to do it some day to amaze a group of friends.

It was this trick Mr. Crenshaw had told Pete about, and which Pete thought Jupiter should know of. As Pete said, he had been unable to sleep and tried to telephone Jupiter, and finding both Jupiter and Bob unaccountably missing, had raised the alarm.

Jupiter was inclined to be annoyed at himself for not guessing that a large mirror could easily conceal several small pictures, but Bob and Pete pointed out to him that he had so brilliantly succeeded in other phases of the investigation that he could be pardoned for not realizing this final point.

In fact, when Jupiter turned on the tape-recorded scream for the first time, he noticed the mirror shiver slightly and guessed what was supposed to happen. By turning up the volume, he was able to shatter the mirror in a dramatic enough manner to satisfy even him.

One point remains. Why did Mr. Clock send the strange messages to three friends, and the screaming clock to the writer, Rex King, instead of just writing to the police? Mr. King himself supplied the answer, which I am sure is the correct one.

To use Mr. King's own words, "Bert knew I was down on my luck and hadn't had a job for a long time. Here in Hollywood publicity is very important. I needed something to get my name in the papers, where movie and television producers would see it and remember me.

"He dreamed up a scheme whereby I would find the missing pictures in a very dramatic fashion, which would be in all the newspapers. After all, if I hadn't been in the hospital when the clock came, I could easily have contacted the others, solved the messages, and taken some reporters and detectives to witness me finding the pictures. It would have been a big story, and I'd have got plenty of publicity.

"Bert was a good friend, even if he was a thief, and the last thing he did was try to do me a favour, so I can't think too badly of him. I'm only sorry it didn't work out the way he planned, because I could use the publicity."

You'll be pleased to know, I'm sure, that the stories in the newspapers did carry Mr. King's name, and that he got several jobs as a result.

As for The Three Investigators, they have put this case in their *Closed* file and are looking for a new one. I can only wonder what it will be!

ALFRED HITCHCOCK.

The Hardy Boys Adventure Stories

by Franklin W. Dixon

The escapades of Frank and Joe Hardy, sons of a famous detective, and their staunch friend, Chet Morton, lead to breathtaking dangers and adventures. If you can't resist a gripping plot, daring heroes, death-dealing villains, hair's-breadth escapes and plenty of action, the Hardy Boys are for you!

Armada

Armada Science Fiction

Step into the strange world of Tomorrow with Armada's exciting science fiction series.

Armada Sci-Fi 1
Armada Sci-Fi 2
Armada Sci-Fi 3
Armada SF 4

Edited by Richard Davis

Four spinechilling collections of thrilling tales of fantasy and adventure, specially written for Armada readers.

Read about ... The monstrous Aliens at the bottom of the garden ... A jungle planet inhabited by huge jellies ... A robot with a human heart ... The terrible, terrifying Trodes ... A mad scientist and his captive space creatures ... The deadly rainbow stones of Lapida ... The last tyrannosaur on earth ... and many more..

Stories to thrill you, stories to amuse you – and stories to give you sneaking shivers of doubt ...

Begin your science fiction library soon!

Armada

has a whole shipload of exciting books for you

Armadas are chosen by children all over the world. They're designed to fit your pocket, and your pocket money too. They're colourful, gay, and there are hundreds of titles to choose from. Armada has something for everyone:

Mystery and adventure series to collect, with favourite characters and authors – like Alfred Hitchcock and The Three Investigators. The Hardy Boys. Young detective Nancy Drew. The intrepid Lone Piners. Biggles. The rascally William – and others.

Hair-raising spinechillers – ghost, monster and science fiction stories. Super craft books. Fascinating quiz and puzzle books. Lots of hilarious fun books. Many famous children's stories. Thrilling pony adventures. Popular school stories – and many more exciting titles which will all look wonderful on your bookshelf.

You can build up your own Armada collection – and new Armadas are published every month, so look out for the latest additions to the Captain's cargo.

If you'd like a complete, up-to-date list of Armada books, send a stamped, self-addressed envelope to:

Armada Books,
14 St James's Place,
London SW1A 1PF